World, Other World

Simon Just

Sometimes one world isn't enough...

Publishers Catalog-In-Publication Data
Just, Simon
World, other world / Simon Just.
p. cm
1. Science fiction, American. 2. Short stories. I. Title.

813.6--dc22

Contents: In a holiday mood—Broken statues—Tenor of Yesterdays—The madness took—Standing up to Nell—Any more normal time—All this indeed—Sympathy for lot—Doze—As strange as most—What if we lose saturday—It was a gesture—The new world—A clean well-lighted cyberspace.

(First Printing, 2008)

SECOND EDITION

ISBN 978-0-9837042-7-0

Cover design: J. Simon

Send Coffee Books
http://www.sendcoffee.com/publishing.html

To anyone who ever called me weird,
whether I heard them or not.

Introduction

The line between general fiction and science fiction is sometimes too thin to define. Often writers trip to one side and find their work included with one or the other group, despite their original intent. In this collection by Simon Just, you'll find some stories in the World collection include characters and situations a little outside of general fiction. The Other World collection includes character and situations that, though distant from us, bring a sense of familiarity in their nature and circumstance.

World

Other World

World

In a Holiday Mood

Jorge was late for work again Thursday, the second time that week. He made it past the boss' office with little effort. He says he has a way of thinking himself invisible, but no matter how many times he tries to explain it, I can't do it. He can stand next to someone, and they don't even see him. It's not that he's quiet. It's a true talent.

"Hey, nice tie!" I called, as he slipped into his cubicle beside mine.

"I just grabbed one." He came around the barrier between our work areas, having shed his jacket. He held up the bottom of his tie. "Don't even remember buying this one." It looked like the busiest Hawaiian shirt ever, made into a tie. "Nelson come through yet?"

"Nope. You're a lucky man."

He nodded and went back to his area. No one noticed he was late Tuesday, either. I'm telling you, this man is charmed. He's been acting sort of strange lately, and just a little, I hope he slips up. He's the golden child around here. I was told all about him when I started a little over a year ago. No sick days taken, no vacation for the past three years. He's like a legend. The rest of us are background.

Wednesday, Jorge finished all his programming for the day in about four hours. Then, he left. I didn't see him till lunch. I was sitting at the table with my microwave soup and corn chips, leafing through some business magazine. I don't even know which one. They all look pretty much the same to me - news about companies I wouldn't work for, and news about companies that would never hire me. Just so many words, but the print ads are great. I like the equipment. I'm slow on programming, by most standards, but I like the hardware.

So, I'm sitting there looking at some new cheesecake shot of a server blade, and Jorge comes in with his lunch. He's got a bag, but not like your standard brown-bagger bag. It's grocery size, and he's holding it flat-ways. He reaches in and pulls out a pineapple upside-down cake.

"Whose birthday?" I ask. Someone usually brings

something when a birthday's near. They always seem to know. Maybe there's a list somewhere, but I've never seen it.

"Did I forget your birthday, Sammy? I would have made up a card for you."

"No. I mean the cake." A few heads look over. Funny how the word 'cake' can do that. There's a word you shouldn't yell in a crowded room.

"Oh, that's my lunch," he said, opening the cake's container, then reaching in the bag for a plastic spoon and knife. "You want a slice?"

"No, thanks. I've never been much for pineapple."

"I forgot to bring something this morning, and on my way here I decided to stop and pick something up."

"A whole pineapple upside-down? That's what you picked?"

"It caught my eye." He pushed the cake towards me. "Scrap off the pineapple and have a slice."

"No, really. I'm good."

Maybe that's not too strange, bringing a cake in for lunch, but I've never seen anyone do it before - not a whole cake.

The next day, Friday, Jorge was right on time. He

came in carrying a Tiki man. It was six inches high, and looked hand-carved. He smiled and said, "Good morning," as he passed me. I had been on my way to reception. I needed more blank Cd's and no one was in Supply, but the Tiki needed investigation. I followed him around to his cubicle.

Jorge set the statue on his desk, then took off his jacket.

"What's up, Sammy?"

So much for my attempt at invisible. He didn't even have to turn around to know I was there.

"You got any blank Cd's?"

He opened a drawer, and I could see a mother-load of blanks. He grabbed a handful and turned to give them to me.

"Nice Tiki."

"Excuse me?"

"The statue. Classic Tiki."

He backed up and looked over at it, ran his fingers through his hair.

"It's a little something I made."

"You made it?" I went in for a closer look. Picked it up, turned it over. No sku label on the bottom, only a 'J' -

for Jorge, I guess.

"Yeah. It's nothing much. I put in some landscape timbers and had a few pieces left over from the cuts. He didn't match the others, so I decided he might look better here."

"The others?" I set the statue back on his desk.

"There were a few cuts I had to make. Couldn't see wasting the ends." He shrugged.

"How'd you... what did you use?"

"I have a little knife. It didn't take as long as you'd think. Nothing really."

When I came in the next Monday, Jorge was already there. He was typing away with headphones on. A lot of us work with earbuds in or headphones on. Years ago, when I worked with people all around my same age, we'd put on a CD or radio station. Now with newer programmers coming in we can't agree, so we pop in earbuds and fire up our iPods. I went to my space and started work. I could have sworn, around lunch, I heard him singing Calypso, unless there's some other song with the line "Daylight come, and me want to go home".

Tuesday, when I came back from lunch, there was a little plastic fish sitting on top of the barriers between our cubicles. I asked Jorge where it came from, but he said he didn't know. Then, he named him Nemo and said he was glad he finally found him.

I asked Michelle at reception if she noticed anything weird about Jorge lately, but she wasn't sure who I meant. I looked at the vacation schedule. I thought maybe he was taking his long-deserved vacation, but his name wasn't down. My name isn't down either. I'm following in his footsteps. If he can go without a vacation, so can I. If he can be the golden boy, then I can at least be the silver boy.

On Wednesday, Jorge brought a Tiki in for me. It was smaller than his and had a lei around its neck.

"Look," he said, as he set it on my desk. "Someone got laid."

"That explains the grin." I said. Though it was good of him to bring one for me, it kind of creeps me out. Not that he made one for me, but the look on its face. It looks like it's laughing, which should make me like it, but it doesn't. It's not like I think it's laughing at me - not really - but like it knows some joke I don't. I turned it around so it was facing the wall. Let it laugh at the wall all day.

Thursday, I started falling behind on my workload. I was trying to get ahead and almost had, but with all the confusing behaviour in the cubicle next door, I was losing my concentration. That's the one thing you need most in programming. You lose your place, and you have to reread a lot of code to remember where you were.

I could hear Jorge singing along with his iPod. I couldn't make out the words, but it was enough of a distraction to throw me off. I decided to take a break and have a sip of water, shake it off.

I stopped by the men's room on the way back. One of the sinks was full of water with a small paper boat floating in it. It looked lonely, out there at sea all by itself. I pushed it back and forth a little - imagined the captain wondering what wrong turn they'd made that brought them to this basin of water, with high marble cliffs. I heard a voice right outside the door, so I grabbed the boat and drained the sink.

Sometime that night I made my decision. I was going to take a vacation. I couldn't be Jorge. For some reason, I simply couldn't do it. Maybe, I didn't have his work ethic. Maybe, I was just a slacker at heart. All I know is, I wanted a vacation. I wanted to lie on the beach, fish off a pier, drink fancy drinks and dance the night away.

The next morning, I headed right to the vacation calendar. Two weeks to this day, I was going to ask off. I flipped to the next page of the calendar. My week was already taken. Paul had the week chosen. The next week was Ahmod's. The week after was our annual corporate training. The week after that was clear. I wrote my name across it.

"Where you going?" It was Jorge.

"What?"

"On vacation. Where you going?"

"I haven't decided yet."

Jorge came in Friday in sandals. Sure, men wear them practically anywhere in summer, but not to the office. He said he stubbed his toe and couldn't get his shoe on. He slapped his way around the office all day.

I didn't feel much like working. I was behind, but no amount of effort would catch me up by the end of the day. Whatever happened to casual Fridays? Jorge obviously still believed in them, if you didn't buy the stubbed toe excuse.

I took off my tie after lunch. It was my own, personal casual Friday. I was unbuttoning the collar of my shirt when Nelson walked up.

"Sam, how are things going?"

"Fine, sir." Without thinking, I reached over and set my hand on my tie. I knew I couldn't put it back on. Like he wouldn't notice that? Maybe, I could scratch my neck, then put it back on, like there was something bothering my neck, and I only took it off for a minute.

"I haven't received all your files for the week yet."

"No, sir. I'm still working on a few."

"You'll have them by the end of the day?"

"Well, a few were giving me some trouble..."

"I'll give him a hand," Jorge broke in. I have no idea how long he'd been standing there. He turned off his stealth device and suddenly appeared.

"Do the best you can," Nelson said.

"Yes, Mr. Nelson." I dropped my head on the desk, as soon as he turned and left.

"Give me a few files, Sammy. I'll see what I can knock off before closing."

Jorge finished most of the files I hadn't even started. He handed them over to me, rather than Nelson. That was kind of him.

"You know, I haven't had a vacation in three years."

"How do you survive?" I asked. I'd only been there a little over a year, and I couldn't take it anymore.

"I take my vacations while I work. I turn myself off, and Nelson doesn't even notice." I looked down and saw he was wearing a pukka bracelet.

"Can you try to explain how to do it, again?"

9

"Sure. We can talk at lunch." He walked away, putting his earbuds in and turning up the music. He was still wearing his sandals, and he walked with a casual saunter of someone with nowhere to go.

I waited for Jorge in the lunchroom, but he didn't show up. Nelson came in and thanked me for finishing my workload for the week. I was going to tell him Jorge deserved a lot of the credit, but I didn't.

He said we were going to be a little busy, could I postpone my vacation a month or two. I told him I thought it would be all right. If Jorge explains his stealthing method, I can take my vacation while I work, right? I looked into Jorge's cubicle later, but didn't see him.

That was a week ago. I haven't seen Jorge since. I figure he might show up again. Maybe, Monday.

Broken Statues

"I don't think they'd be like that if they had a childhood like mine," Emily told Caitlin. A group of slack-panted, obnoxious teenagers had just come through the diner, making sure everyone was well aware of their presence. They talked louder than necessary, accenting their thin conversation with harsh words best left to the imagination.

Emily and Caitlin were finishing their lunch. Caitlin glanced down at her lap, a quick check for loose crumbs. Emily contemplated her coffee, lost for a moment in some stray childhood memory that, to her, stood in sharp contrast to the life these kids must know.

"But you said yourself, times were tough for you." Caitlin looked around Emily to where the kids were sitting.

"Sure, but tough breeds character. Tough produces ingenuity."

"Oh," Caitlin smirked. "Like the ingenious idea of running a bike tire around with a stick? I'm pretty sure they invented that in the twenties."

"Hey! They used a wooden ring. Don't knock it. Do you have an old bike tire?" Emily pushed her plate aside, clearing away for the idea forming in her mind. "Wait. Maybe I do. I could--"

Caitlin interrupted, "I am not trying it. It was fun, fine. I take your word for it."

"You'll never know, unless you try it. It's all about balancing the tire with the stick, while keeping it spinning..." Emily's eyes shifted upward, as though watching the image in her mind. She looked back down and gave a small chuckle, acknowledging her tendency to get carried away.

Caitlin glanced over at the teenagers. They'd settled down some.

Emily followed her gaze. "It's odd," she told Caitlin, "how one looks so much like the other."

"It's called fashion or trend at least."

"I couldn't follow trends when I was their age."

"It wasn't about clothes so much back then,"

Caitlin said, tapping her straw against the few remaining cubes in her tea.

"Back then? What school did you go to?"

Caitlin smiled, "I guess, I just took clothes for granted."

Caitlin knew, though they'd been friends for nearly ten years, they were miles apart in their upbringing. At times she felt jealous of the simple life Emily remembered growing up, though they were only a year apart in age.

Caitlin's life was filled with riding lessons, piano lessons and weekends at the river. Emily's was filled with exploring the woods behind her small house, growing tadpoles into frogs, planting gardens, and reading. Caitlin had gone from a hectic childhood to a hectic adulthood, with barely a chance to stand still for a breath. She was better equipped for the real world, having lived with one foot in it almost all her life. However, the differences in their childhood had given Emily a chance to see the world from an angle Caitlin had not.

Emily decided long ago what was fake and what was true, what mattered and what could fall to the wayside. She was hard to shop with, pointing out styles that would last only a season. She didn't read the throwaway books Caitlin devoured like candy to a toddler.

At other times, Caitlin thought her friend Emily a braggart. Emily told how she and her dog walked through the woods at night. Caitlin heard in this a criticism of her own fear of doing things alone. When Emily showed her a blouse she still wore, which belonged to her mother when she was younger, Caitlin heard that she was not thrifty, or that she had no grounding in her past. Somewhere, between those two emotions, Caitlin knew that Emily only hoped to share with her the joys she had as a child. Like the child who still shown through in her eyes, she had no malice or even moral to her tales.

"Caitlin?" Emily broke the stare that Caitlin held on her tea glass.

"Sorry, ready to get back to the grind?" Caitlin reached for her purse.

"I was going on again, wasn't I? Well, stop me next time."

"No, I was thinking, about a week ago our lights went out for nearly two hours. I thought to myself, what would Emily do?"

"Light a candle and get on with life?"

Caitlin nodded, and smiled. "That's just what I did."

"Speaking of getting on with life." Emily grabbed her purse and nodded toward the door. They left to return to work.

Caitlin sat at her desk after lunch, thinking about the blackout. Rather than light a candle and get back to her life, she had first panicked, then called the power company, then panicked again. The darkness inside seemed stifling. Finding a flashlight, she went outside.

When her thoughts truly came around to what Emily would do, she imagined Emily and her family without electricity for nearly four months. Caitlin looked over her shoulder at her own house. She would never survive.

Emily had made it out to be a grand adventure - lanterns, candles, actual ice blocks in the refrigerator, and kerosene heaters against the cold. She imagined Emily's family, huddled around the heater. Emily's mom reading to the children by candlelight. How cozy and warm it must have been. Had they talked all night, told stories? What must have daylight been like? Light filling the night-darkened rooms again. Finding the barrette you lost in the dark the evening before - given up to the night.

Sitting outside in the cool air, Caitlin imagined herself as a child, in wonder of the night sky. She thought of herself, small, young, having no electricity, perhaps never again. But, she told herself, a child wouldn't think in terms of 'never again'. A child would be there, in the moment, enjoying the moment. A child would adapt. She looked around her small yard. A firefly flickered by her. It wouldn't be so bad, for a child. Children don't have to worry if the food will spoil, how they will wake themselves for work in the morning. Caitlin tried to push the adult concerns aside.

She got up from the steps and walked to the garden, shining the light from one flower to the next. Another firefly lulled past, and she reached out and took it in her hand. Opening her hand, she let it walk across her palm and onto the back of her hand, before flying off. She laughed despite herself. Even on vacations as a child, her mother scheduled her so tightly she'd never had time to stop and catch a firefly.

She turned off the flashlight. Everything was black, but for the small points of light blinking on and off all about the yard. Her eyes traced the dots of the moving constellations floating around her. A light breeze toyed with her hair. She reached out her arm and pointed, trying to guess where a firefly would blink next, laughing when she missed, as though the firefly had tricked her.

A click, then rushing sound, broke her train of thought, as lights broke the darkness. Caitlin heard her television come back to life, a car commercial shouting about the latest, no-money-down sale. Reluctantly, she looked down at her flashlight, clicked it on and off, and went inside.

Caitlin's computer beeped with a message, bringing her back to the present. It was an email from Emily asking her to call later. She looked up at the clock. Only a few more hours to go and she was off for the weekend.

Emily stopped by her mother's house on the way home from work. She visited for dinner at least once a week. After their meal, as drank their coffee, Emily's mother asked about Caitlin.

"She was teasing me again about the bike tire I played with as a child," she said. "She thinks it's silly, but I may just get a tire and make her try it."

"You and that tire. I wish I could have bought you real toys," her mother said.

"I liked it. It was fun."

"I suppose you liked not getting more than one gift at Christmas - if that?" her mother asked.

"I didn't mind. You made us those dolls one year."

"Made from old bits of cloth and curtains. I couldn't afford anything new. Those were horrible, ugly dolls, too." Emily laughed. Her mother frowned. "That was a good gift to you?"

"Yes. No one had dolls like that. They were special. You gave me one of Grandmom's broaches once. I still have it."

"I'm surprised it hasn't turned to dust. It's ancient costume jewelry."

"I love it."

"You had such a horrible childhood. Old clothes, no real toys, no electricity at times."

"It was fun. It was an adventure."

"It was hell. We were so poor. It took all my effort just to make due."

"But, we made due."

"Barely. It was a house of cards, ready to go at any time."

Emily looked at her mom in disbelief. "But... you never let on. You always made it fun."

"It was all I could do. I hated having to put you kids through that. There are times I can't believe we made it." With that, Emily's mother took her cup to the kitchen. "When you finish your coffee, put the cup in the dishwasher."

The clicking of dishes and the running water faded into a steady drone, as Emily sat in her mother's living room seeing her childhood from an angle she had never imagined.

World, Other World

The Tenor of Yesterdays

I woke up to the sound of a low rumble outside. It was only about an hour after I'd gone to bed. I went to my window and looked out. The sky was dark blue, because the moon was almost full, and thin, wispy clouds covered most of it. Through the clouds I could see planes. From the sound, I would say there were hundreds of them, but I could only see two or three. They were large planes, not airline planes, and they were flying very low. I ran out of my room for the kitchen to look through the back door.

My dad was standing in the kitchen by the counter. He didn't seem surprised to see me. The back door was open and, before I could ask what was going on, the screen door opened. A man in a military uniform stepped into the doorway. Dad looked over. He wasn't surprised by this either, so I guessed the man had already been in our house.

"There will be a slight concussion," the military man said. Dad just nodded. They both looked over at me.

"Sam, this is Colonel Swenson," Dad said. "There's a little problem in the canyon. Nothing to worry about."

My brother, Matt, and sister, Molly, came up behind me. Matt looked over at the kitchen window, then at the colonel. He ran over to the window. Kneeling on the seat, he pressed his face against the glass and used his hands to shield the kitchen light from his view.

"What are they doing in the canyon?"

"They're in the canyon?" Molly ran over to the window beside him.

"There's a problem in the canyon," Dad repeated.

"What kind of problem?" Matt asked. "That's our canyon! They can't just go in there without us letting them!"

"Matt," Dad said, "the canyon isn't ours. It's not part of our property."

Before Matt could protest further, the colonel stepped to the side of the door and a woman came in. She wasn't dressed in military clothes, but black pants and a berry-coloured turtleneck.

"Mr. Wells, this is Olivia Cohen. There's," the colonel paused and looked at Miss Cohen, who offered him no help, "a substance in the canyon, we need to check your home. It can... leak into the surrounding area and we need to make sure your home is safe." Dad nodded in agreement.

"I'm going to have a look around. This probably won't make much sense, but I can feel the..." she glanced at the colonel, "substance. I'll just go through the house, pick up a few things. I'll try to do this as quickly as I can."

"What sort of substance is it?" Matt asked. The colonel glanced from the woman to Matt.

"It's like uranium," he said.

"Then why don't you use a Geiger counter?" Matt asked.

"It's like uranium, but it's not uranium," the woman answered. She looked up at Dad. "Do you mind?"

"Not at all."

"I'll start here then." She walked over to the stove and ran her hand over it. She touched every knob, the elements, the handle, all with a swift passing graze. The cabinets, sink, and drawers got the same treatment. Every cabinet door and drawer was opened and she ran her hand over the front of each.

23

On the counter, she ran her hand over a catalog, stopped, and picked it up. She quickly leafed through the pages. I walked up to Dad, not because I was afraid, but because I could see what she was looking at if I stood right beside him.

The woman stopped on a page in the catalog and ran her hand over it. Her fingers lingered for a second on the image of a blue and white, crocheted afghan. She rubbed the image lightly, then closed the catalog.

"This," she said, handing the catalog to the colonel. He took it and handed it through the door to another military man standing on our back deck.

I looked over at Matt and Molly. I thought it was funny that a catalog would be contaminated, but they didn't seem to think so. I could tell by their faces; they knew more about this. They didn't want the woman to find whatever it was she was looking for.

"How many times have you been in the canyon?" She was asked Matt and Molly. They looked at each other. Molly looked down.

"A couple times," Matt said.

"And you, Molly, isn't it?" she asked.

"The same," Molly answered. I knew Molly and Matt were lying. We lived by the canyon for more than a year, and they went there almost every day. Dad knew it to, but he didn't say anything. Maybe he was afraid they'd take Matt and Molly away. I was afraid they would take us all away. The woman looked at me.

"I've only been there once," I told her. That was the truth. I could feel Matt and Molly's gaze. They didn't know I'd ever been in the canyon.

I was eight-years-old when we moved to the house by the canyon. Dad said it was more like a dry gorge, but my brother Matt liked the way *canyon* sounded, so the name stuck. It was really little more than a cut in the earth. The walls were about ten feet high, but to an eight-year-old the gap seemed to go down forever. Loose boulders lay in the bottom, so you couldn't walk through that area even if you found a way down. A small winding path ran down a ledge on each side. It was covered with boulders and loose stones, but there was enough space to walk. The paths were ground level, with rock walls six feet higher on either side of them. Molly and Matt would go exploring for hours on end. After months of begging, Dad made them promise to stay on the paths and not go very far. I wasn't allowed near it.

The year before we moved to the canyon, my mother died in a household accident. That's what they called it. Dad said she was just balancing her checkbook before she went out shopping and didn't realize she shouldn't do it with the car in the garage and the motor running. Everyone was very sympathetic, but Dad kept saying if we had an alarm or a detector in the garage, maybe it wouldn't have happened. Dad wanted us to start over someplace new, so he moved us out of the city. He quit his job with the paper company and got a job with the Forest Service. He said he used to work with paper, now he was working with the trees. He called it 'getting back to basics'.

Part of his plan to keep us safer was making sure we were ready for any emergency. He had a wall in the kitchen lined with kits and alarms. There was the usual first aid kit, but also a blackout kit and a fire kit. The fire kit was the best. It was a box shaped like an arrow that pointed to the front door. The glass lid of the arrow box glowed a pale blue. Dad said sometimes you can't see too well in smoke, and you might get turned around. The light would show us how to get out. All the boxes had a small toggle-switch on them. If we needed a bandage we would take it, but if it was something really bad we were supposed to hit the toggle. The box would call 911 for us. It was something he wired up himself. He was very proud of his emergency boxes. He did his best to make sure we were always safe.

The one time I had been in the canyon was only a few days before the colonel and the woman showed up at our house. Molly and Matt were leaving for one of their explorations and I decided to follow them, a few feet behind. They always acted like the canyon was their secret place and I couldn't understand or appreciate it. They told Dad it was too dangerous for me, so he agreed that I shouldn't go, but Dad wasn't home that day, and I wanted to find out what they did for hours there.

It was a hot day and the rocks seemed to absorb the heat and radiate it. I would duck behind a boulder, watch where Molly and Matt went, then run a few feet and hide again. I was keeping up with them pretty well, till we got about halfway. When I peeked out from behind a rock, they were gone. I stepped out onto the path and waited. They didn't show. I thought I caught a glimpse of Molly one time, but when I ran up to where she had been, I couldn't find her. I walked the path all the way to the other side of the canyon. There was a small house on the other side, but no sign of Molly or Matt.

I sat on a rock and waited to see if they'd show up. A boy came up. He was only about six.

"Hi," he said. "I'm Troy. Where'd you come from?"

"Over there." I motioned towards the canyon.

"You live in there?" He kicked the stones with his worn tennis shoe.

"No, silly. I live on the other side of the canyon."

"Oh. You like gerbils?"

His mom let him show me his gerbil and we talked about TV shows we liked. I told him I'd try to come back again sometime, but I wasn't supposed to go through the canyon. He said his dad called it Fire Gorge, and he wasn't allowed there either. It was getting dark, so I left.

I was only about halfway back through the canyon when I realized why I shouldn't be allowed in there. It was a long walk, too long for me. The sun was setting, and I wasn't sure I would make it home. I thought I saw a flashlight up ahead, so I ran to catch it. If it was Dad I was in trouble, but if it was Matt and Molly I could probably get them not to tell. The light blinked around and always seemed just a few feet beyond. Before I knew it, I could see my house, but the light was gone.

The woman cleared the kitchen and living room. She passed a cabinet knob and our TV antennae to the colonel. She made her way to the back of the house, to our bedrooms. Now and then she'd call out 'This' and come out holding something for the colonel to take. One time it was the doorknob to our linen closet. The colonel had to get someone to bring him a screwdriver to get it off.

"Sorry about this, Mr. Wells," is all he said as he carried it out. Dad shrugged. It was getting late, and we were all tired.

A coin, letter opener, a bunch of rocks, and a CD case later, the woman made her way to my room. That was when we felt the explosion. Me and Matt and Molly raced over to the window. There was a cloud of dirt over the canyon. Miss Cohen came out of my room to have a look.

"Don't be startled," the colonel said. "They'll likely do a few more. We should be able to take care of this in short time."

Lights rose out of the cloud of dust, just like the flashlight I had seen that day coming home through the canyon. I thought it was the military men making sure they'd done whatever it was they were doing, until the colonel pulled out his walkie-talkie.

"What the hell are those lights? Do you have men in there?"

"Negative, Colonel," came the reply. The colonel left quickly.

"I'm quite sure that's everything," Miss Cohen said. She followed the colonel out. That was the last time we saw them.

When we got up the next day the canyon was surrounded by a large fence. We tried to find a hole to peep through, but couldn't. Even the top was covered. We'd hear noises. Sometimes trucks, but they must have gone out the other side, because we never saw them. Molly and Matt tried walking around the fence to the other side, but someone who looked like a lumberjack stopped them. He told them they were trespassing and had to turn around. I asked Dad what could be going on, but he didn't have an answer.

I think it bothered Matt and Molly that they couldn't go into the canyon anymore. Molly spent most of her time playing with a keychain. She'd hold it in her hand and close her eyes. I only know, because I peeked in her door once. Matt had a part from his bike that he played with the same way. They'd been like that since the canyon was blocked off. I didn't understand it. Then one day, I went to open my window.

It was the first nice spring day. Dad always scolded me for opening the window using the frame. He said I would knock the wood off and the glass would cut me. When I reached for the window, I remembered not to use the frame. I grabbed the sash lifts. As I touched the one on my left, I got this weird sensation. It was like I was floating right above myself, but it wasn't scary. I pulled my hand away. If I put my finger right over the lift, without touching it, it felt like it does when you touch the TV screen when it's turned on. Something told me this was what the woman felt when she took stuff from our house.

I touched it again, thinking about the canyon. Everything got foggy. Then, I could see inside the canyon. It looked just like it did the only time I was there. I could see the sun and feel the heat from the rocks. The smell of fall and first fires in fireplaces filled my senses. It was like I was reliving that moment in time. Pulling my hand off the sash lift, I tried to think of something else. I thought of my last birthday and touched it again. My whole birthday party played out before my eyes. I could even taste the cake.

I went to the kitchen and got out my dad's tool box. It took me a while to get the sash lift off. It had been painted over a few times. As long as I thought only about getting it off, I wouldn't drift off somewhere else. It was like you had to focus on something to make it work.

When Dad came home, I went in my room and got the sash lift.

"Why don't you sit down, and I'll help Molly make dinner?" I said.

"That's too big a job for the two of you."

"Come on. I have something to show you."

"What is it?" He put his keys on the hook and hung up his jacket.

"You have to sit down." He could tell by the grin on my face that I was up to something. It made him smile. It had been a while since I saw him smile. He walked into the living room and sat down.

"Okay. You didn't break something, did you?"

"Nope. This is cool. You'll see." I held the sash lift behind my back. "Hold out your hand, and close your eyes." He did. "Ready?" He nodded.

"What's your favourite memory of Mom?" I asked him, then slipped the sash lift into his hand.

The Madness Took

I stepped out of the side door of the house and took minimal refuge under the overhang. I lit up a cigarette and looked around. Large snowflakes were falling, thick as an old sweater. Won't last much longer, I thought. I'd been told, the larger the flake; the faster it passes. A clump of mingled flakes plopped on my head. It went straight to my scalp and began to melt, a small stream running down my face. All around me, walls of white.

The bells of the church down the street began to chime. What was the song? Was it Come All Ye Faithful? It seemed I was missing every third note, so I couldn't tell. I stood in the midst of the snow and listened to the two notes I could hear, imagining the third at its turn.

The door I'd escaped through, opened. Russell popped his head out, looked around, then at me.

"Scott? What are you doing out in the snow?"

I held up my cigarette as an answer, but before a word could leave my mouth, Franklin pushed passed him onto the patio. It was a graceful passing, considering Franklin's large build, not a heavy man, but stout, with a presence extending beyond his size like a force-field. Russell, though tall, was lean and moved aside as a bush gives way on passing.

"I imagine he's enjoying some wonderful tobacco." Franklin reached into his pocket and pulled out a cigar. He nodded towards me, then looked back at Russell. "You can join us, Russell. I have a few spares hidden throughout my clothing."

"Too strong for me, thanks," he replied. They both looked over at me. I was new to this group, having just started at the University a little over a month ago and knew Franklin and Russell mostly in passing, but I understood the look. It was the same look you get when you pull out a pack of gum in a group. I reached in my jacket pocket and pulled out my cigarettes.

"Would you like one?" I tapped a cigarette to the top of the pack. Franklin extended a light. "I didn't know you smoke."

"He's a chipper," Franklin said, clicking his lighter closed, a vague lingering smell of fluid in the air.

"A chipper?" I had never heard the expression.

Russell exhaled in little puffs, a ring of smoke with each.

"I smoke about three cigarettes a day, often less, rarely more."

"You seldom hear the term," Franklin said. "Doesn't really support the whole 'cigarettes are highly addictive' campaign."

"Science, or those who wield it, refuse to see anything that doesn't support whatever they hold as their current notions." Russell said.

"I heard a doctor once say, 'I won't tell you the percentage of smokers who develop lung cancer. If I did, you might take up smoking'." Franklin smiled and took a drag from his cigar.

"What is it?" I asked.

"What? The percentage? A couple percent: three, five, not that they have any real proof in that."

Russell nodded in agreement.

"Then," I started, "why don't we hear that

anywhere?"

"No one wants to be the modern Galileo," Russell said. Franklin chuckled a bit.

"The Tobacco Inquisitions," Franklin said. "I can see that happening." Franklin turned to me. "You can't trust scientists. Surely, you know that by now."

"We have no imagination," Russell added.

"Party line, all the way." Franklin made a smooth gesture with his hand, running it forward like a plane taking off. They both snickered.

"Our kind are known to be bought. We fudge the numbers. We beat down anyone who has an idea different from what we currently hold as true," Russell added.

"So, you're fudging those percentages?" I was sure they were trying to pull a joke on the new fellow.

"We're renegades." Franklin motioned towards Russell. "Some day we'll write a small pamphlet with our theories and print it out ourselves."

"We'll send copies to everyone we know," Russell said.

"Then, we'll be ostracized, vilified, and eventually..."

"After our death," Franklin interjected.

"We'll know great fame." Russell pulled his jacket around him. The wind had picked up since we first came out. The snow had all but stopped, with a small flake here and there floating perpendicular as though it was running past us.

"I'm going in," Russell said. He looked at Franklin's cigar. "Blink that already, will you?"

Franklin pulled a tiny case from his pocket and withdrew a small cup. He rolled the end of his cigar into the cup, then put the cigar and case in his jacket.

The cold followed us into the house. A ghost of air rushing in around us. A few heads turned towards the door as we entered, then returned to their companions.

"I'm going to the bar. What can I get you two?" Russell asked, shaking the cold from his jacket.

"Gin and tonic," Franklin said, with no hesitation.

"I'll have the same." One drink was as good as another to me. I'm not much of a drinker, but I've learned that carrying a drink is easier than explaining all night why you don't have one.

"Liquor's okay, then?" I asked Franklin.

"And candy's dandy," he replied.

"I mean in science. Same rules apply? Truth be known?" I thought perhaps they were simply explaining their own vices away.

"Red wine is good for you... wait, no, it's bad for you. On second look, it's good for you. If you're an alcoholic, you can never have a drink again. Wait, no, you just need some self control." Franklin shrugged. "I'm still trying to sort out if coffee is good or bad for me this week. I have to struggle with that every morning. Turn on the news first thing to make sure I can have my cup."

Franklin gave a small wave over my left shoulder to someone. I turned and looked.

"I hope she doesn't come over," he said this through his teeth, as though he feared she may read his lips.

"She's in the English department, isn't she?"

"Yes," he replied, looking off over my right shoulder. "I don't want to mind my grammar this evening. She's a stickler. Ah, here's my man."

Russell walked up carrying a drink in each hand, the third squeezed between them with barely fingertips to balance it. Franklin took his drink from the center. Russell handed me my drink.

"What are we debunking now?" he asked.

"What have you got?" Franklin asked.

"Is that your hobby, then?" I asked. "Going against

the current wisdom?"

"We're tomato eaters," Russell said. Franklin laughed. I shook my head. I had no idea what he meant.

"The general public," Russell said, "used to believe tomatoes were poisonous, till some brave soul..."

"Colonel Robert Gibbon Johnson." Franklin raised his glass as though to toast him.

"He ate them for an audience to prove he wouldn't die."

"If, in fact, that is even true." Franklin turned to me. "So much of what we believe to be true, could very easily be rumors of old. There are still those who believe the world is flat."

"There can't seriously be..." At this point, I was sure they were either pulling a prank on me, or they'd had several drinks before I ran into them on the patio.

"Look it up!" Franklin glanced around. He leaned towards Russell. "Are they walking food around, or do we have to hunt it down?" Russell put a finger in the air. I turned to follow his view and saw a vested server nod in acknowledgment.

"On the way, old boy - not that you'll starve."

"We like to eat the tomatoes," Franklin ignored Russell and continued, "tip the sacred cows. We like to find the Fessendens, the Wegeners, the tiny voices trying to shout above the din..." Franklin said.

"And steal their ideas and get the credit," Russell finished.

"We are the Edisons to their Teslas!" Franklin and Russell touched glasses and drew them up to empty them.

The server came up with the tray. Franklin grabbed a stuffed mushroom and popped it in his mouth. He made a pleased sound, put his empty glass on the table beside him and took three more mushrooms. I took two, and Russell declined.

"Would you like another drink, sir?" the server asked.

"Gin and tonic, good man."

"I'll have one sent over."

Russell set his glass on the table. "Bourbon and water." The server looked my way. I lifted my almost full drink.

"I skipped lunch," Franklin apologized for his appetite. "What else have you?" He asked the server.

"Brie baked in puff pastry with apricots, new potatoes stuffed with spinach and bacon..."

"Sounds good. Ask them to make a run by us, will you?" Franklin's hand grazed the pocket on the server's vest. I caught a glimpse of a bill, of unknown denomination, though the movement was so slight I would not have noticed had I not been looking down at the tray. The server nodded and withdrew.

"Our latest project," Franklin began but stopped, pulled a handkerchief from his jacket and wiped his mouth and hands. He stuffed the cloth back into his pocket. "Excuse me. Boorish of me, really, but I haven't had a thing since breakfast."

A young woman in a server's uniform walked up with a tray of drinks. She spun the tray gently so that two glasses, settled together, were facing Russell and Franklin. They took their drinks with a nod, and she floated off, the drinks barely registering her footsteps.

"Where was I?" Franklin took a sip of his drink. "Oh, yes. Evolution."

"You mean to invent evolution?" I asked.

"We mean to disprove it." Russell took a sip of his drink.

"Not that it's ever been proven, really," Franklin added.

"Neither of you seems to believe anything has been proven, as yet." I was beginning to see them as

41

bored men, amusing themselves with a belief they could test the norm.

"The history of science," Russell said, "is filled with paradigm shifts and each time a shift occurs, it is trumpeted with the expression, 'We now know'."

"We now know. We now know the earth is round. We once believed the universe was finite, infinite, a box on the desk of God - but we now know..." Franklin trailed off.

"If science really knew every time they claimed they did, there are no atoms, no germs..."

"And all we are, all we are made of, are four bodily liquids."

A server appeared with a tray. Franklin took only two of the small pastry puffs it contained. I took one, biting a bit to make sure it was not something distasteful, but on tasting it put it in my hand with my drink and took another.

"Much of what Freud professed is now being ridiculed," Russell said. "It may come back in fashion again, but for now he is not as revered as he had been."

"Are you saying evolution is just of a fashion?" I asked.

"It's barely 150 years old. Tomatoes were thought

to be poisonous for longer than that." Franklin washed down his pastry and glanced about for the next server.

"Most of the examples used to prove the theory of evolution are simply examples of natural selection," Russell said. "If, say, food was available only in a tree where the tallest could reach it, only the tallest could eat, live, breed. The race would grow taller. That isn't evolution. It's simply natural selection."

"And never - never - has unprecedented genetic material showed up in any mutation," Franklin said. "A frog can be born with an extra eye, but never a wing. Remember that. It disproves even the possibility of evolution, that simply."

The server with a tray of potato puffs emerged from my left, startling me.

"Sorry," I told the server. The conversation put me a little on edge. They were trying to convince me that everything I was taught was merely someone's, or some group's, current fancy of how things work. I was more comfortable with the idea of things being settled.

"Could I get a gin and tonic, please?" I asked the server, taking a potato puff from the tray.

"These are good," Franklin told the server. He smiled politely at Franklin and nodded. "Russell, try one. Seriously good for a bit of potato and fluff." Russell took the puff and tasted it. "Good, right?"

"Yes. For an hors d'oeuvre, it's good." He put the last piece in his mouth and brushed his hands together.

"He doesn't like hors d'oeuvres," Franklin told me, picking another off the tray.

"They just make me hungry for real food. They're like taking a small bite from everyone in the room's plate."

"Please. And you'll go home and eat a frozen dinner, won't you?"

"But, it will be all mine." Russell smiled and took a sip of his drink.

Franklin nodded the server on, popping a last bite in his mouth. He washed it down with a large swallow from his glass. "So, what do you think, Scott?" he asked me.

"About what, which part?"

"Think you'd like to be a tomato eater, too?" Franklin gave Russell a small grin.

"I don't think I'm up to the challenge. I'm liberal arts. I don't have the background to contradict established scientific theory."

"Accepted theories," Russell said. "They're not

really established. They're just accepted."

"All the same, it's not my area of expertise."

"You don't have to challenge them. All you have to do is not accept them."

The woman server came up with my drink on her tray. Franklin reached for it, but stopped himself.

"No, go ahead," I told him. "I have to leave soon, anyway." He took the drink and set down his empty glass. I set mine beside it.

"All it takes is a sense that no one really knows." Russell said. "When you see something about... say, dinosaurs. Do you know how many actual skeletons they have? A little over 2,000."

"And many made from a single piece of bone or a tooth," Franklin added.

"You're suggesting I be skeptical?" I asked.

"Oh no, it's more than that." Russell said. "They don't know. They don't know that some odd beast existed sixty-five million years ago from the tiniest piece of bone. It's a matter of realizing they don't know. No one really knows."

"They've found non-fossilized dinosaur marrow in some bones. Sixty-five million-year-old marrow?" Franklin asked.

"True," I said. I remembered a mention of that in the news. I hadn't paid much attention at the time. I didn't realize the improbability that it was really as old as they said and yet non-fossilized. To me it was only an interesting story. It conjured the hope, and fear, of an actual park of cloned dinosaurs.

"Then, you'll join us?" Franklin asked.

"I'll defend you to the press, when the time comes," I told him. Franklin and Russell laughed. "I should get going." I nodded to each of them and made a step away.

"Next time," Franklin said, "we'll discuss whether it's warming or cooling we should worry about." I smiled and made my way to the door.

As I walked to my apartment, the snow started again. I tossed about our conversation in my head. Come to think of it, I only heard the report of the marrow once. It seems something of that importance would have been remarked on all over the world. It would turn the current dating system on its ear. I'm a little surprised it hasn't been mentioned more. I may ask around, see who else has heard it.

Standing Up To Nell

It had been three weeks since Abigail and her new husband moved into Melinger Manor. Abigail was excited to take hold of the responsibilities of a house. When they first married, a little over three months ago, they lived with her husband's mother. It was not an uncomfortable situation, but similar to living at home with her own mother taking care of her.

When they married, Abigail and Herman came to the decision she should stay at home. She never had a career, just a string of meaningless jobs, so she liked the idea of not having to work. There were to be children in their house, though they still could not agree on a number. Abigail was an only child. She thought a houseful would be wonderful. How many times as a child had she wished for playmates right there in her own home? Herman was from a family of six brothers. He thought two children would be best.

Melinger Manor had been in the family for years, but closed-up for the last ten. A great-aunt was the last to live there. Once she passed on the family had no use for it. When Abigail and Herman announced their engagement the house came up, but was in such disrepair it took almost two years to make it habitable. The plumbing, wiring, and appliances were all updated. Abigail expected to walk into a fully modernized mansion, but the contractors were hired only to update fundamentals. Walls were still in need of painting, wallpapering, decorating.

When they walked through on the first assessment, Abigail noticed the new finish on the hardwood floors, but the gas fixtures from a previous century were covered with dust and fingerprints of the workmen who removed long forgotten pipes. Herman noticed Abigail's intent on them.

"Just a wall fixture now," he said. "Nothing to worry about. We can leave them up, or take them down. Entirely up to you."

"Leave them," Abigail said, trying to sound as though she didn't care, but knowing he would not believe her attempt. She had made a great fuss about the fixtures when they first saw the house. Somehow, she thought, they might leak.

"The pipes are shut off," Herman told her.

"But the kitchen, it still uses gas, and the dryer. The pipes are all connected. How can we be sure none will leak into these fixtures?"

Somewhere to the back of her mind sat the thought that Herman had come into the house the day before and set all the fixtures askew - marking them with his own fingerprints to settle her mind.

The first two days in the manor - and it was a manor, large and old - were spent with sheets over furniture while friends and family helped paint and clean. This was Abigail's idea. It was easy enough for Herman to pay someone for the work, but with such a large family, many who were intrigued by the manor and had last been there as children, it was like a reintroduction.

The great-aunt who owned the house was mostly a hermit, seldom taking company. A few relatives had looked around the house after her death. Two of Herman's brothers even considered the house themselves, but the age and condition were beyond their means. Bringing them all together for painting and cleaning as a group effort would be gratifying.

Herman disliked the idea immensely. He thought it just a bit of her girlishness. Being twenty years her elder, he wrote off many of her ideas as silly. Herman didn't look his age, or at least that's what Abigail told herself and anyone who would listen. He was a good, stable man with her best interest at heart. This belief she would also impart on all who'd hear her.

Contrary to Herman's belief, the house warming party was a success. The women went about cleaning and chatting, while the men took to the paintbrushes like old friends. Almost all the women were career women. Something in the simplicity of cleaning seemed like a break to them. A spot on the floor was easier to tackle than a client who wanted to take a plea that wasn't to his advantage. The final evening ended with a barbecue on the patio behind the house.

Abigail's many sisters-in-law stopped by for days afterwards, offering a hand or a hint. With their help, Abigail moved and re-moved furniture - what little they had of it. A stereo here, a chair there. The back living room, as the house held two, was simply a sofa and stereo. Abigail hung a large print of a café scene over the fireplace, but Herman insisted a print wouldn't do. They would have to pick up something more fitting for a house of this stature. Abigail argued the stereo system, with its many attachments and buttons was not altogether appropriate either. Herman quoted the cost of the system as his argument.

The visits slowly stopped. After two days with no one coming by, Abigail had a slight sense of relief. The flurry was passed, and now she was in her home. Herman left early to drive into the office. The gardener and his crew arrived about an hour later. Abigail sat in the kitchen nook, drinking her coffee and watching the team of workers trying to make something garden-like out of the jungle of a backyard. She wondered what she would do with herself. Everything was clean. Everything was painted, put into place, stored away or still yet to arrive. The dining room table wouldn't arrive for another two weeks. Without it, she had no idea what the dining room would look like. She had gone through all the catalogs, marked pages, and now had to wait for the furniture before she could make final decisions on incidentals. Herman had told her not to get carried away with the furnishings. The next day a truck pulled up and delivered an outdoor grill the size of their sofa.

A grating noise came from the back living room. Abigail set down her coffee and slipped out of her chair. She went to the doorway of the living room and looked in. The large sofa was no longer in the center of the room, but over by the wall opposite the stereo. She stood in the doorway and stared at it. She looked over at the French doors leading to the patio. They were closed. As she stood in the doorway, the sofa moved, only slightly, but closer to the wall. Abigail turned and ran. Grabbing her car keys, she flew out of the front door.

She stopped on the porch. Where would she go?

Had she really seen it, or was it her imagination? She looked back at the door, then sat down on the porch stairs, clutching her keys tightly. If she had thought to grab the phone, she could call Herman and tell him something strange was going on. Doubtless, he'd have an explanation. Standing up, she looked into the front living room window. She could just see the doorway to the back living room. Moving to the side a little, she caught a glimpse of the corner of the sofa - centered in the room. "Could that have been my imagination?" Abigail decided she would meet Herman in the city for lunch, rather than go back inside to find out.

As she expected, Herman explained she was simply overly stressed with moving, decorating, and the thought of being in the house all day with nothing to do. He suggested she get a hobby.

"I'm sure I saw it," she told him.

"I'm sure you believe you saw it," Herman told her.

"It was almost all the way to the wall."

"Perhaps, there's a tilt to the floor. I could have the foundation checked, but I thought the inspector took care of that. If I had a level, I could check it myself."

"Maybe, I could do some window shopping and follow you home after work?" Abigail was not far enough away from the incident to write it off completely.

"I'm going to be late tonight. Don't be silly. Just go home, straighten up a little. Leave some dinner in the microwave for me, in case I don't feel like picking up something on the way home."

Abigail stopped at a hardware store and bought a level. She wasn't sure what to do with it, but having something that may explain what she saw gave her confidence enough to drive back to the house.

When she got home, Abigail went in the door, leaving it open. She walked cautiously into the front living room, glancing from side to side through the doorway to the back living room. The sofa was in the center of the room. Nothing looked out of place. She closed the front door and steadied herself. Quickly walking into the back living room, she placed the level on the sofa and left. A loud clunk rang through the house. Frozen, Abigail tried to remember if she set the level on the edge of the sofa, or towards the back of the seat. She stood, waiting to hear another sound.

Knocking startled her. Someone was at the front door. It was the gardener. They needed a crane to pull down an old oak tree. They were leaving for the day to hire one, and they'd be back with it in the morning. Relieved that her overactive imagination may be to blame, she went to the kitchen to decide on dinner.

There were no sounds that evening, except the sound of Herman coming in late. She heard him turn off the lights she had left on for him to find his way through the house. He muttered to himself prior to each click of a switch. Before he made it up the stairs, she had already fallen back to sleep.

In the morning, Abigail made Herman his breakfast, and waited till he'd left to throw away his dinner from the previous night. The gardener and his crew arrived while she was loading the dishwasher. The rattle and groan of the crane filled the house with sound, which in a way was comforting. If any strange noises were to come from the back living room, she was sure not to hear them.

Making her way through the house, she opened windows to let the spring breeze and sounds surround her. Down the stairs and through the dining room, she strolled past the kitchen into the back living room. Unlocking the French doors she opened them, pulling each out at an angle to welcome in the sun. She stepped back to look at the scene she had set. *"If the garden wasn't in disarray, and a crane wasn't there, this would be a wonderful view,"* she thought. She took another step back. Something touched her arm, and she felt herself being pushed off to the side. She spun away from the pressure and tried to dash out of the room, but hit a block - a wall, a force, something in her path. Turning again, she ran to the French doors, out and around the corner of the house.

"Good morning, Ma'am. Did the noise startle you?" The gardener was standing by his truck, drawing water from a large cooler on the back.

"No, it was just... a spider. I don't like spiders."

"Would you like me to get it for you?"

"Thank you, no. I'm sure it's run off."

"Most of them really won't harm you. Only a few you have to look out for."

"How is the oak tree coming?" She put her hand up to shield her eyes, squinting towards the crane.

"Almost out. You know, there'll be a large hole when we pull the stump. If you're considering a pond..."

"I'll have to ask Mr. Melinger."

"Of course. If we get that far today, we can move on to something else and fill the hole tomorrow, once you know."

"Are there any plants worth saving?"

In place of a reply, the gardener yelled out, "Miguel!". A young man ran up to the gardener and he motioned and talked quickly to him, while Abigail considered making her retreat.

"Mrs. Melinger?" The gardener had sent the young

55

man off with his instructions.

"Yes?"

"There's a butterfly bush that's in wonderful shape and a few rose hedges you could consider moving somewhere closer to the patio. Let's have a look."

Abigail stayed in the garden for the rest of the day. She walked with and without the gardener over the property. It was a large backyard. The gardener had told her the dimensions, but the numbers meant nothing to her. She asked about a central grass area, a place children could play. He showed her the layout Herman had suggested, but told her he could easily make changes at this point. She deferred the decision to Herman. It was his family home, and he was paying to have the work done, so she didn't see that she could make changes to what he had requested.

When the gardener and his men left, she walked over to the large hole left by the tree stump. It was over six feet across and looked quite deep. Standing beside it, she looked up to the house. It was neatly centered, and a good distance from the back of the house. If it were a pond, it would be far enough away that small children wouldn't wander into it, but could be seen from the upstairs windows. She would ask her husband that evening. Reluctantly, she made her way back to the house, without the support of the rumbling crane or crew of workmen only a shout away.

Abigail went in through the kitchen door. She started for the refrigerator to find something for the night's meal, but stopped quickly. There was music coming from the back room. *"Perhaps, Herman left the stereo on when he went to work and I didn't notice with the noise of the crane?"*

Moving slowly to the kitchen table, she sat down. She drew her hand to her mouth, biting her nails - a habit she had broke herself of years ago. *"I could simply walk in there and turn it off."* The thought of something she could not see, touching her, drew a shiver. *"I could make dinner and enjoy the music."* She tilted her head to the side, but couldn't see into the room from where she sat. *"I'll turn it off and start dinner,"* she told herself, standing - then again, with every step towards the door.

Reaching the door, she hurried into the room and hit the power button on the stereo. It went off for a second, then came back on again. She hit the button again. Again it came on, one station, then another in quick succession.

"I want this off!" she shouted, pushing the button again. The stereo stayed off. As she turned to leave, she was shoved, not lightly, but not enough to bring her down. She was jostled, again. Something, someone, was pushing her towards the kitchen. She helped them -

bolting the rest of the way on her own. At the door she stopped. The presence was gone. Both feet squarely in the kitchen, she waited. Nothing happened. No sound. No shoving.

As she made dinner, she hummed a tune to herself. Whatever it was - and it was *not* her imagination - it didn't want to enter the kitchen.

When Herman came home that evening, she asked him about the pond, but didn't mention the incident in the back room. He was sure to say she was imagining it, or worse think she had lost her senses. She talked about the garden and the possibility of a pond. He didn't like the idea of a pond at all. "Too much upkeep. Mosquitoes will breed in it." She nodded with his comments, but in the morning she told the gardener he was still considering, and could they not fill the hole for a few more days? She asked the gardener about mosquitoes, and he told her if she had fish they would eat the larva. That evening she told Herman fish would eat the larva, but he still thought it was a bad idea.

Abigail made it her morning chore to open windows, and her nightly chore to close them all. There were too many hours to fill, and the gardener was working too hard to answer her every question. One morning, as she was about to come downstairs from opening the top floor windows, she glanced over at the attic door. If there was any window up there, it would surely need to be opened.

She went through the door and made her way up the stairs. Expecting spiderwebs and dust, she put her hand out in front of her, but to her surprise it was mostly clear. New piping and spare shingles were lying by the top of the stairs. The workmen who fixed the house had been up here. There was a small window off to the far end. She made her way to it and was glad it opened easily. Perhaps, the workmen used it to vent some heat. Looking around, she noticed a stack of boxes off to the corner. She decided to have a look.

Most of the boxes were very old and held books of all sorts. There were gardening books, which she set aside to take downstairs with her, and a cookbook or two, but there were also many old fiction books. These she left as they were. One box looked fairly new. She pulled it open to have a look. Inside were personal effects - a hairbrush, a handkerchief, some bottles of perfume - most empty - and a journal. Settling down on a box of books, she opened the journal.

'Nella May Johnson' the inside page read. Nella May was the great-aunt who lived in the house some ten years ago. Abigail flipped through the pages. The dates went from one month to the next, one year to the next. The last few pages had entries written years apart, as though the author would lose the book for some time, then come across it and start anew. She picked a page at random.

"Today someone called for me, but I didn't answer the phone. I don't like the phone. James liked to talk on the phone. I should get rid of the damned thing like I got rid of him."

Abigail was shocked, not only did she not know the great-aunt was married, she now wondered about the circumstances of the loss of her husband. She moved on to the next entry. It was written six months after the last.

"I didn't cook tonight. James always said I didn't cook enough and I was trying to starve him. I'm not the cooking kind. I read a book today. It was good. It was better than cooking. It was better than just about anything James ever wanted me to do."

Abigail laughed to herself. *"What had James wanted her to do?"* She flipped a few pages and read another.

"Maybe, if I had been a better wife James would still be here. Maybe, I should have listened better. But, I'm happy. I was never so happy as the day he left. I couldn't take any more of him telling me what I should do every minute of the day. You want to keep a man - you cook for him. You want to keep your sanity - you tell him to cook for himself."

Abigail laughed out loud. She put the journal on top of the other books she'd collected and carried them downstairs.

That evening, Herman asked Abigail if she knew why the hole in the yard had not been filled.

"I thought we were still considering a pond."

"I don't think it's a good idea. It could bring in vermin to drink. If you want a bird bath, that's fine."

She was sure he was simply putting his foot down to hear it stomp. No one could be so terribly against a pool of water in their yard.

The following morning Abigail pulled out the journal to read more. Aunt Nell had been a very strong woman. Sometimes she thought this was her best asset, other times her worst flaw. As Abigail read the entries, she was inspired by the conviction of some of Aunt Nell's strengths and saddened when she read her doubting herself. Nell's writing always seemed at its best when she was full of spunk.

"You're quite a character, Aunt Nell!" Abigail exclaimed aloud. As soon as the words left her mouth, she heard the grinding noise of the sofa sliding across the floor in the back living room. She rushed to the doorway, in time to see it stop.

"Is that you, Aunt Nell?" Abigail asked quietly, almost embarrassed to say the words. The stereo sprang to life. Abigail stood at the doorway, looking around the room intently, trying to see if there was any physical sign of anyone, anything, in the room.

"I won't have this," Abigail said quietly to herself. She took a deep breath to steady herself, but could feel goose bumps rising on her skin.

"I won't have this," she said again, a little louder. The stereo changed stations once, then again.

"This is my house now." She was almost shouting. Abigail's body started to shake, from fear or anger she wasn't sure, but she walked into the back room.

"This is unacceptable!" Abigail shouted now. Her body was alive with chills, and a ringing of fear was in her head, but she stood her ground. The sofa moved towards her. She put out her hand and stopped it.

"You listen to me, Nell. This is my house now, and I will do as I please in my house. You had this house, but now you need to move on, and let the living live!"

Abigail felt something come up beside her and nudge her towards the kitchen door. She stood firmly, the ringing in her head nearly drowned out by the rising volume of the radio.

"I will not leave this room until you've heard me

out. I will go wherever I damned well please in this house, and you will either accept that, or leave. You were a smart woman. You should know when you've met your match. I've read your journal. You were right to stand up to James. He was a brash bully. If you behave as he did, I will stand up to you!"

The stereo went silent. Abigail stood, still shaking. She was too frightened to move, but held a brave, proud expression. The sofa moved ever so slightly, back to its original spot. Slowly, the French doors opened, and Abigail looked out into the vast backyard leading up to a large hole.

That evening over dinner, Abigail told Herman they were indeed going to have a pond.

World, Other World

Any More Normal Time

Henry stands by the back door of his house, wind gently rustling his hair. A woman, his wife, is in the garden with her back to him.

"Honey, are you okay?" he asks. She turns to face him, catching the loose hairs wisping around her eyes and gives him a weak smile.

"I'm fine. How are you?"

"How am...?" he starts, confused by her response. "It's just - you've been standing there awhile."

Holding her hair back with one garden-gloved hand, she brushes her work jeans with the other.

"Oh, I'm just waiting for the wind." She turns away from him, crouches down. Picking up her trowel, she lightly tosses some soil.

"Can I get you something to drink?" Henry asks.

Without looking up she calls over her shoulder. "No. If I get thirsty the garden hose is right here." She motions off to her side.

"Anna, dogs drink out of hoses, not people." There is a hint of frustration in his voice.

"We don't have a dog, Henry."

Stunned by her logic, Henry shakes his head, turns and goes back into the house.

After a few seconds, Anna sneaks a look over her shoulder to make sure he's gone. Sure he's well inside the house, Anna raises her head to the sun and wind and closes her eyes.

"When will you stop?"

Henry, standing aside the kitchen window, watches her. *"We don't have a dog,"* he says. His shoulders drop, as he runs his hand over his head, looking failed. There's a knock at the door.

"Henry? Anna?"

"Come in, Ed. I'm in the kitchen," Henry calls.

Ed comes in carrying a brown paper bag. "I've got more tomatoes for you," he says. "Stella said Anna wasn't having much luck with hers, so I brought you a few extras we had."

"Get you a drink?" Henry goes to the refrigerator and looks inside.

"Sure, it's a really hot one today. Glad for the breeze."

Henry pulls two bottles from the refrigerator and opens them on a can opener on the wall beside it.

"Good time for a gardener to take a break, when the wind kicks up a bit," Henry says.

"Cools you, but can scatter your seeds." Ed takes a sip of his drink, brings the bottle down. "Speaking of which, your son Tom still scattering his seeds all about town?"

Henry laughs. "No, he's taken up with Bonnie's kid, Chelsea," he says. "Claims it's serious this time." Ed laughs. They've both heard that before from Tom. "He'll settle down soon. I told him you were thinking of hiring him on with you, but he says insurance is just a racket."

Ed looks up, not so much offended as amused. "And what's his career choice?"

"Marketing." They both laugh.

Henry puts his bottle up to toast Ed's. "Wouldn't know a racket if it bit him on the ass."

Anna is on her hands and knees pulling out weeds and talking to herself, humming between her talking.

"You think you're pretty, but you're a weed. Can't fool me. Not again. Weeding fool. Garden tool. Weed garden. I should plant a weed garden."

She stops. Rising to her knees, she looks around the area.

"What do you think?" She asks the plants. "One garden for all of you? A nice home - or a place for you to fight it out. Let the strongest survive. Weaklings fail. Weedy weaklings. Weedy weaklings fail."

She looks down and starts to cry. She pulls off a garden glove and tosses it down. From her back pocket she pulls out a tissue, quickly dabs her eyes, then blows her nose. She looks around, shoves the tissue back into her pocket and puts her glove back on. Anna starts humming again and pulling out weeds.

Ed and Henry are sitting at the table talking. Henry is pulling tomatoes from the bag Ed brought over.

"These are better than last years," he says.

"Yeah, unbelievable crop. This weather's been good to them. Don't know why Anna's having trouble." Ed takes another sip of his drink.

Staring at a tomato as he turns it in his hand, Henry mutters, "She keeps moving the plants."

Ed looks confused. "Moving them? What do you mean? After she already put them in the ground?"

"Yeah, one spot's too shady, one too sunny and she thinks they'll burn..."

"Sun's good for 'em," Ed says.

"One spot is too wet. One too dry. There's always a reason." Henry sets a tomato gently on the table and looks toward the window. "They haven't spent more that a week in the same hole."

"That won't do. Is she out there now?" Ed gets up and goes to the window. He looks out on the garden area. Anna is motioning to a plant with her trowel.

"Maybe I should talk to her?" Ed says.

Henry hurries over. "No, no, don't worry about it. If she's happy moving them around... well, it's her garden."

Ed looks puzzled, turns to Henry standing beside him. "Is she talking to that plant?" Henry steers Ed away from the window.

"Yeah, it's something she read in a gardening book. Least she's not blasting Mozart through the neighborhood." Henry forces a laugh. Ed laughs, politely.

"I should probably get back. Stella is getting things ready for the market tomorrow morning. She'll think I'm just avoiding helping her." Henry walks Ed to the door. "Think you and Anna will make it out to the market?"

"We'll try."

Anna gets up early. Henry brings up the market, but Anna says she isn't up for crowds. She dresses in her garden clothes, an old pair of khakis covered with grass and dirt stains that never came out through washing, an old shirt with matching stains. She comes into the kitchen. Henry is drinking his coffee.

"Do you need a hand out there?" Anna is putting on her gardening gloves. The smell of mosquito spray fills the house.

"No." Anna goes to the kitchen drawer where they keep odd things that have no special place. She pulls out a roll of twine and digs around in the drawer.

"What are you looking for?" Henry asks.

"Scissors."

"They're in the bathroom. I forgot to put them back." Henry gets up to retrieve them, but Anna is already headed down the hall. He sits back down.

Anna comes back from the bathroom, walks

through the kitchen and into the backyard without a word. Henry takes his coffee to the window.

Anna unrolls a long piece of twine. Measuring it against a large drooping bush, she cuts the length, and carefully pulls it around. Holding the ends, she gently pulls the bush upright and wraps the ends around the closest tree. She gives the twine a tug and ties it off.

"Posture is everything." She runs her fingers through the long strands of branches. "This year you'll bloom." She senses Henry's gaze. Avoiding a glance back to the house, Anna picks up the twine and shoves it in her back pocket. Grabbing the scissors, she cuts a small branch from the bush.

"Stop watching me," she says, cutting another. "I can't stand you watching me." Anna snips the bush randomly, then stops cutting and drops the scissors. She looks around the garden, pulls her gloves tighter and walks over to another area.

The phone rings. Henry answers it.

"Hello? Just a minute, Claire." He sets the phone down and goes to the door.

"Anna, Claire's on the phone for you." She doesn't respond. "Anna? It's your sister." She doesn't even look up. Henry goes back to the phone.

"Claire, she's working in the garden right now.

Can I have her call you back? She's fine. No, really I think she's doing all right. Maybe you could call back around noon. She'll probably be in for lunch. All right. Bye." Henry hangs up the phone.

Anna grabs handfuls of peat from a large bag. She tries to toss it into the hole she's dug, but the wind keeps blowing it out of her hands. She drops the peat and sits back on her knees. Holding her head up to the wind, she closes her eyes, and waits. The wind dies down, and she quickly grabs more peat and tosses it into the hole. Picking up a potted plant, Anna takes the stalk in one hand and pounds the bottom of the pot with the other. The plant breaks free. She picks up her trowel and cuts through the web of roots at the bottom. Dropping the trowel, she squeezes and pulls the roots free, sets the plant in the hole, and fills the dirt in around it. Anna turns to get the hose, but it's not there. She looks around, stands up. A gust of wind whips her hair. A bee buzzes by.

"I just had it." She spots the hose and walks over to it. Taking off one glove, she grabs the hose with her gloved hand and sprays her bare hand. Bringing her wet hand up to her hair, she runs it lightly over her stray strands of hair, plastering them to her head. She dries her hand on her shirt and puts her glove back on. Pulling the hose behind her, she walks back to the newly laid plant and waters it.

"Anna?" Claire stands beside the garden watching Anna dig violently at a long, large root.

"Yes?" Anna doesn't look up. She trowels around the root more, pulling up and digging under it.

"What have you got there?"

"A root."

"I see that. Do you need a hand?"

"I have two." Anna twists the root backwards and uses the trowel like a lever to pry the root free. It snaps, throwing her back. Claire runs over and puts out her hand to help. Anna pushes herself up. She throws the root towards the woods.

"Are you okay?" Claire asks, looking her sister over.

"I didn't get it all."

"You got most of it."

"Most of it, doesn't count." Anna brushes off her pants and turns to face Claire. "Why are you here?"

"I came by for lunch. Henry thought it would be nice."

"Henry thinks a lot of things. Henry thinks Tom will straighten out. Henry thinks I move the plants too much. Henry thinks the bills pay themselves. Henry thinks I worry too much. Henry thinks we're happy."

"Anna, please."

Anna brushes her hair back. She looks around the backyard. "What do you think of my garden?"

"It's pretty. I like it," Claire replies, without looking around.

"I put in a few things since you were here last." Anna points to the plants with her trowel. "That's a Bush Clover. Those are Scotch Brooms. You should come by when they're in bloom - quite a spectacle - waterfalls of colour."

"They sound lovely. Henry said you've been working very hard out here."

"You know, I've never really been happy with Henry." Anna walks away, picks another spot and kneels down to pull out some weeds.

"Anna, you don't know what you're saying." Claire follows her. "You love Henry. You have since the day you met."

"Never did."

"It's just a bad time for the two of you. He's getting used to the new job. You're trying to work out a new budget. Tommy will come around. He'll find his bearings. It will be fine." Claire kneels down beside her sister. "It will all work out. You'll see."

"I only married him because it was all too much at the time."

"What was too much, Anna?"

Anna digs violently at the weeds, pulling them out and tossing them towards the garden paths.

"Momma passed away. You were off and married. Daddy was ill. I didn't know what to do. I wanted somewhere else to be."

"Anna, stop saying that."

"I wanted it to be better. I wanted things to be calmer."

"He loves you, Anna. You know that."

"That's what bothers me the most." Anna gets up and moves to another area. Claire goes after her.

"You can work it out, Anna." Claire watches her sister pulling recklessly at the plants. "It's a little tough right now. Why don't you and I go somewhere for lunch? We could talk."

"I thought marrying him would help." Anna rips out a plant. She looks at it, then sticks it back in the ground. Pushing stray dirt around the stem, she tamps it down with the trowel. "I thought any change would be good."

"You two were so happy. You can be happy like that again."

A strong wind twists Anna's hair, slapping it around her face. She tosses down the trowel and rises up to her knees. "You see?" she says. "It doesn't stop. You think the winds have died down, then here they come again, knocking everything about. There's no where safe."

"Come on in, Anna." Claire crouches by her sister. "We can figure this out, together."

"Will you tell him? Tell Henry I don't love him?"

"No, Anna. I won't. It's not true." Claire stands up.

"Okay, then. You're right. It's in my place." Anna stands up. She glances towards the house. Henry is standing by the back door.

"You ladies ready for lunch? I made us soup and sandwiches. That sound okay?"

Anna pulls off her gloves. "Yes, Henry, that sounds lovely." She smiles up at him and shoves her gloves in her pocket. She looks over at Claire. "I'm sure you're right. It will all be fine." Anna walks towards the house.

All This Indeed

Riley Moore was having a hard time concentrating. He sat in his customary spot at the library and shifted his position again. He looked up at the lights. They were no more or less bright than on previous nights. The room was no more quiet or noisier than usual. In fact, the library was much the same as every night he came, still and comfortable. Those were the two things he liked best about it. Those, and the smell one could find by the reference books. It was the woody, slightly musty, but inviting scent usually found only in older homes. He would always make a pass of the reference books on his way in, and often thought if they could bottle the essence, he's sure he'd find a perfect mate in its wearer. Once, on a whim, he had purchased a cologne based on the scent of ink, so was paper really so strange? What would be a more perfect match?

He set his mind to the page once again. After reading the same sentence for the third time, he sighed. He couldn't clear his mind of his conversation with Dylan earlier in the evening.

Dylan, Riley's ne'er-do-well cousin, had come to stay with Riley while he got 'on his feet'. After several weeks with him, Riley realized Dylan was rarely on his feet, especially late in the evenings almost every night, when he was barely able to walk. Dylan liked to go out, liked to meet new people, liked to sometimes bring them home with him for the evening. When Riley protested, Dylan would do his best to charm and cajole him. Usually this worked well, as Riley sometimes stayed at the library till closing and never knew of the guests till he bumped into a strange woman mulling about his kitchen in the morning.

This was the life Dylan believed Riley should share as well. When Riley protested and tried to explain the appeal of reading, Dylan mocked and ridiculed him. After any one of these arguments, Riley often found himself wondering if Dylan could even read. He had placed books about the house, hoping Dylan would pick one up. He didn't want to convert Dylan to his lifestyle, just to let him see the joys he found in reading. Not to enlighten him, but to get him to end his frequent assaults. Had today's discussion been like the previous ones, it wouldn't have weighed so heavily on Riley.

Usually Dylan started with a stray comment, "You read too much. You should get out more." Then he would slowly escalate his charge to a fevered pitch, talking over Riley's replies so that one charge could not be answered before the next was thrown. However, this afternoon Dylan remained calm and listened to Riley's account.

"There's so much to see in the world, and what I can't see in person, I can read about," Riley explained.

"But what about the actual seeing? Wouldn't that be better?" Dylan had countered.

"I lived the life you're living, when I was younger and my liver could take it. Now, I live through the books."

"But, only through the books."

"I go out on occasion"

"To a book discussion? To a museum?"

"Yes," Riley told him. "I go to museums to see the artifacts of the civilizations I've read about. It makes them more real to me."

"We live in a civilization now. What do you know of that civilization?" Dylan scoffed.

"I know it has good libraries." With that comment Riley had felt for the first time since Dylan had come to live with him, he may lose a discussion. In others, Dylan had ranted till he was through, then walked off in a huff. He quickly saw his weakness and added, "Do you know what it's like to live on Mars?"

"Of course not."

Riley went to the bookshelf and picked up his copy of the Martian Chronicles. He handed it to Dylan. "You might find this interesting."

Dylan set the book aside. "Do you know what it's like to see a pretty lady from across the room and know she'll be coming home with you that evening?"

"You can't know that from a glance."

"Oh, but dear cousin, you can."

"A woman who'll be gone in the morning, never to be seen again."

"All the better."

"And each night another? After a while, are they all really so different?"

"Different enough," Dylan shrugged. "And yet same enough that it's almost like a marriage."

"That's nothing like a marriage!"

Dylan laughed. "Defending an institution to which you yourself have never committed?"

"I would, if I met the right lady."

"A librarian?" Dylan laughed again.

Riley would have preferred arguing to being scoffed. "Certainly not the ladies - women - you bring home."

"Have you ever talked to any of my women? They could be quite intelligent."

"You yourself don't know if they are. The most I've heard from any of them was, 'Can you call me a cab'. Perhaps, they don't even know how to use the telephone."

"I just think you should get out more," Dylan said, almost quietly.

Riley tasted a concession. He hoped they had finally reached an impasse, and these exchanges would come to an end.

Dylan looked down at the book Riley had given him. "If I read one of your books, any one you choose, will you come out with me one evening?"

Though it was a small price to pay, Riley could see the whole evening flash in his mind - his cousin showing him about to the ladies, like a hermit coming to see first light. Sitting at a table, listening to them go on about people they know, their work, mocking patrons as they came in and out of their usual hangout. The evening would end with an awkward attempt by his cousin to talk some strange woman into going home with him. In the end it would probably be just he, used as a crutch, to help his cousin along the street and into the house.

"I'll think about it," Riley replied.

Dylan believed he had won the discussion. He put forth the olive branch, and Riley all but accepted it. A self-satisfied smile stayed on his lips, while he dressed to go out. A little too much cologne, and he was through the door, headed to his haunt, ready to size up the women to find one who might give poor Riley a chance.

The crowds came and went, as Dylan drank on. The bar thinned when the before-the-event crowd left, then burst again with the after-the-event crowd. The event could be anything from a movie, to theatre, to even a party somewhere else. Friends waved, sat for a minute, or bought Dylan a drink. He was king of the domain, in his eyes.

Another regular, a woman Dylan wasn't sure how well he knew - had he taken her home once? - came up to the table. "Hey Dye, you seen Tony?"

"No. Not this evening."

"He was gonna meet me. Guess his missus kept him in." She shrugged and walked off with a slight sway, not of womanly, but of fermented devise.

The crowd was finally gone. Only a few stray souls remained. Someone sidled up to Dylan.

"You want to go somewhere else?"

Dylan turned to the woman. Not the prettiest girl he'd seen that evening, but far from the worse. Her eyes were glazed a bit, from whatever the glass she was clutching held.

As Dylan looked in her eyes he saw a bit of himself reflected in them. She thought them kindred spirits, or maybe she thought nothing at all. Maybe she just wanted to escape from reality for a little while, and take him along for the journey.

Dylan mustered a low, "Sorry." He set down his drink, paid his tab and left, unsure where he was going. He just wanted to walk. If that woman was escaping reality with her drink in her hand and her proposal to a stranger, what was he himself doing? Was he living the wonderful exciting life he put forth to his cousin, or was he merely escaping reality, like his cousin, but in a different way? He turned the corner and headed back to his house.

Riley still couldn't read. Between looking at his watch and glancing about, he'd all but given up. *"Why do I need to know the time?"* he thought, as he shook his sleeve over his watch. *"Because the cafe closes in an hour,"* came the reply from somewhere in his mind. He closed the book on his lap and looked over at the clock on the wall. "An hour," he said aloud.

Dylan walked in the door of the house. The dull of the night's drinks seemed to have cleared, and in its place was determination. To what end, he wasn't sure. He looked over at the television, then toward the kitchen. Neither appealed to him. He looked over at the bookshelf. *"Maybe,"* he thought. *"If I read just one, only one, I would have something else to think about."* He walked over to the shelf, his eyes running quickly over the titles. *"Nothing too complicated. Something I could discuss with Riley and maybe some of my companions. I'm sure one of them must read. A classic or something current."* He reached at random and pulled a book from the shelf. Leafing through it to get a sense of the style, he took it to the sofa and sat.

Two hours passed as Dylan read, never looking up from the pages. When he did, he realized his cousin wasn't home. He wondered if he should be concerned, but couldn't remember what time his cousin usually came in. Most evenings he was upstairs already and had never taken note. He decided not to worry for at least a little while longer and continued reading.

At the cafe, Riley sat at a table drinking his coffee. He had brought his book with him to have some company. The cafe was nearly as quiet as the library. The seats were comfortable enough, and having his coffee while he read was a treat. He found himself able to concentrate, and had read nearly twenty pages in when someone approached his table.

"Good book."

Though it didn't strike him at first as a question, Riley said, "Yes," and looked up. A pretty woman stood at the edge of his table.

She smiled shyly. "I'm sorry to interrupt. It's just... I read his first book, but haven't gotten around to the second."

"I recommend it."

"You aren't very far in, though," she said, leaning over to see where Riley held his page.

"No." Riley smiled. "But I like what I've read so far. Does that count?"

"Better than the first?"

"I'd say - better use of description."

"Really, how so?" the woman asked, taking a seat across the table from him.

World, Other World

Other World

World, Other World

Sympathy for Lot

"Daddy, on the trip to our new home, will we see Earth?" Denton asked, as he helped his sister Hannah pack their playthings into a large box for their trip. Denton's father looked over at his wife. She nodded.

"Yes, Denton, I suppose we will," he replied. He had told his son and daughter stories of Earth. He had told them of the war to end all wars fought without a single weapon and everyone was taken prisoner. He explained to Hannah and Denton that he and their mother had come here to escape Earth. Now, fearing Earth may find them, they were moving on.

"Allison," the father said, "the Transporters will be here very early in the morning, is there anything else you need me to take care of tonight?"

"Not unless you can calm my worries. No matter

what you tell me, I still have trouble trusting Transies," she said, running her hand across her forehead, tired from days of packing.

"It's not a matter of trust Allison," he sighed. "It's a matter of need. The Transporters need the minerals, and we need transportation and supplies. The Colonists in Serinus have had no problems with the Transporters, and the mining operation is running smoothly." The father looked up to see how occupied the children were.

"You know it won't be long before Earth finds us. They're searching for everyone who opposed their Universal Government. Our opposition was well known," he whispered to his wife. "This move will be the last. We'll be far enough away. Earth will never find us. They don't even suspect the Transporters aren't mining the minerals they sell."

"But Mark, what if one of the Transies tells someone? Tells them they have renegades mining?" Allison closed the full box she had packed, and started another.

"Allison," Mark said, bothered by how she continued down the same avenues of worry again and again. "Why would any of them tell? Our colony will mine more minerals than they ever could on their own, and all we ask in return is relocation, and minimal supplies periodically."

"Daddy," Denton called. "Hannah and I are finished with our stuff. Do you need some help?"

"No, Denton, we're just about finished ourselves," his father replied. Allison closed another finished box and stood.

"Come on Hannah, Denton, it's time the two of you went to bed. Tomorrow's going to be a very busy day." Hannah took her mother's hand.

"Mommy," Denton asked. "Can I please stay up and have Daddy tell me some Earth stories? Just a little while, please?"

Allison relented. "Okay, for a little while. I don't want you to have bad dreams again." She looked toward her husband. "Not too strong, okay?"

"I promise," Mark answered, heading into the living-room with his son.

Lying in bed, Hannah looked up at her mother sleepily. "Mommy, when we see Earth, will they see us?"

"No, honey," her mother said softly. "They'll never even know we're there."

"Will the place we're going be nice, Mommy?"

"It will be all right."

"But, not like here, right?"

"I'm sorry honey. It won't be as nice as this planet, but we'll make it seem like home."

"Okay." Hannah smiled, closed her eyes, and drifted off to sleep.

Allison made her way back to the dining room to check the cabinets one last time. Their furnishings could not be taken with them on their voyage, there was not enough space, and Allison was afraid something would be left behind. She could hear her son and husband in the living-room. She emptied the last cabinet onto the table to pack.

"But Daddy, everyone thinks differently. Hannah and I are brother and sister and we don't think alike. Why does Earth want its people to think alike?" Denton asked.

"They believe they have found one way of thinking that is better for everyone. In a perfect world, a perfect thought would work, but Denton, this isn't a perfect world."

"Daddy, will our new home be perfect?"

"No, but would you want it to be?" his father asked. "Would you want to think like Hannah, or have Hannah think like you?"

Denton considered it for a minute. "I don't think

that would be much fun. Hannah says some funny things sometimes, but I wouldn't want to think like her all the time."

"Well, it's late," his dad said. "Run off to bed, and dream about our wonderful adventure tomorrow."

"Daddy, I'll miss this planet," Denton said as he rose and rubbed his eyes. His mother stopped packing and looked up toward the living room. Mark stood and ruffled his son's hair. He looked over at his wife.

"It's okay, so will I," he said.

Allison looked down. She swallowed hard and called out, "Denton honey, I'll be in to check on you in a few minutes."

"Okay, Mommy," Denton said as he went to his room.

Mark walked up behind his wife and put his arms around her waist. "It's going to be all right, Allie," he whispered in her ear. Allison closed her eyes and dropped her head backwards onto her husband's chest. She put her hands over his and tightened her fingers around them.

"I was just getting use to being here, Mark," she sighed. "No friends or relatives, none of the conveniences

93

we had before, but I wasn't afraid to think, or dream. Now we're leaving, taking a big risk, entering a new society . . . " She turned in Mark's arms to face him. "This is the only thing we can do, isn't it?" Mark tightened his arms around her waist.

"It's either this, or wait for them to find us."

In the morning after breakfast the boxes were moved into the living-room, and final checks were made throughout the house for any possible stray items.

"Well, Allie, looks like we're ready," Mark said. "Let's hope they show up on time."

A sudden knock at the door startled Mark and Allison. Mark went to a side window and glanced out. "Looks like a transit van." He moved to the door. "Yes?"

"We're trying to find Rio Claro," came a reply from outside.

"Did you make a left or a right?" Mark asked through the door.

"Left."

Mark turned and smiled at Allison. "It's them!" He opened the door. "You must be Ben."

"Mark, it's good to see you. Is everything ready for us?" Ben asked.

"Good to see you, yes. It's just these boxes here," Mark said, showing Ben into the house. "How far away is the shuttle?"

"It's down the mountain a ways. We told them we need a little fresh air," Ben said. "The van will ride right into the back of the shuttle. They never check it. They don't want to tick-off us 'Transies'; not many people are willing to have the job we do."

"Why are you?" Allison snapped. Ben knew she didn't trust Transporters, but he didn't mind, didn't really care.

"Same reason you're leaving here, Ma'am," he said, heading toward the door. "No one wants Earth breathing down their neck." He stepped out onto the porch. "Betty!" he yelled. "Open up the back. We're all set here."

Allison was glad Betty had come along with Ben. She seemed okay, even thought she was in the transportation business. Hannah and Denton came running in the front door.

"Mommy, can we help?"

"No, they can take care of this," she said. "Why don't we tell the mountain goodbye?"

The children took their mother's hands and headed for the door. Allison glanced over her shoulder to catch her husband's eye, but he was busy helping Ben with the boxes.

"Good Morning, Betty," Allison said as she passed. Betty smiled understandingly.

"It's never easy leaving a home behind," Betty said. "But we'll have a smooth trip."

"Run along children," Allison said. "I'll catch up." The children ran ahead, skipping and jumping in the air.

"Betty," Allison said, crossing her arms at her waist. "What are the colonies like? I mean, really?"

"They're all right, as far as communities go. I've never really fit into a group situation." Betty laughed a little. "That and the damn brainwashing Earth believes in is what sent me up..." She looked toward the sky. "But if I were to ever tire of transportation, I'd sure as hell settle there over any other place." Allison nodded as though to thank Betty for the reassurance. Betty shrugged and headed toward the house.

Allison watched her go, then turned toward their yard and gardens. She looked over the area she had called home for almost nine years. The children had known no other. Once she had lived in an Earth city. She had lived in a city with millions of others. She had fallen in love and married, but during that time the changes started taking place. She had been told, as was everyone, that all things must be accepted. You must understand everyone. Everyone is equal. From there, the process moved to only accepting certain points-of-view, all others were heresy.

At times, you were afraid to speak to anyone, not knowing if the current social rule would make your words unacceptable. People were sued, fired, jailed, for 'assaulting' others with words. Allison's spirit had not been broken. She and Mark knew when they came here, it could not be permanent. Earth was not very far behind.

About a year ago, through the renegade network, they had heard the Universal Government decided to bring all the renegades back. Earth feared the renegades would some day return and cause others to rise up against the society. Jail terms and psychiatric care would await any strays found and returned. Renegade children were placed in special schools to retrain them for their place in the new society. The thought alone made Allison shudder.

"Honey?" Mark said from behind her. "The van's packed. Do you want a minute more?" She turned to face him.

"No, Mark," she smiled. "I'm ready."

A short time later, the van safely locked down in the shuttle and everyone strapped into their seats, the shuttle lifted off and headed to their new home.

Once beyond the planet's atmosphere, Ben called out, "All right everyone, you can get up and walk around while we get things ready for the long trip." Mark and Allison took off their seat belts, and tended to the children.

"Hannah, Denton, don't touch anything unless Ben or Betty say you can," Allison told them. Denton ran up to Ben's chair.

"Mister," he said. "When do we get to see Earth?" Ben swiveled his chair around to face Mark and Allison. He nodded toward a large observation window.

"Well?" Mark asked his wife.

"Come children," Allison said, taking their hands. "Let's see Earth." She walked with them to the window. The children watched the window shade slowly rise, revealing a large, blue and green globe which filled most of the window. Over its horizon hung a smaller, gray, mottled globe.

"Mommy, that small one, it looks like our moon!" Denton said excitedly.

"Yes, Denton, it does," she said.

"And the other?" he asked.

Mark drew his wife close as she wiped her eyes

and tried to answer.

"That's Earth, son," he said.

World, Other World

Doze

Lucas needed some sleep. He was three days without. Low on cash, there was no Dreamer for him. The rich could afford a Personal Dreamer. He didn't even have the cash for a REM Shop. It would have to be back-alley Doze.

Since his liberation from Duncan-Morse, he'd maxed out his friends for sleep hours, and they wouldn't take his calls. His boss at Duncan-Morse made it sound like his liberation was the best thing that could happen, but no matter what new term they come up with, he was still fired. Most newly liberated people go straight into REM work till they find a new chore, but he'd been a Rounder too long. He didn't have a cycle anymore. Living off other people's sleep for so long set you up for deprivation, if you couldn't find a source. Duncan-Morse had in-house Corporate Sleepers for everyone on staff., but he wasn't on staff anymore.

Lucas tried sleeping the first day of his liberation. He didn't own a bed, so he lay down on the floor and closed his eyes. Two hours and several fitful tosses later, he got up. Sleep was something he hadn't done since he was fourteen, when they first started selling STATS. The Sleep Time Assimilation Transfer System was held up as the panacea of modern society. Twenty-four hour markets and global trade had made sleep a thorn in the side of every working man.

Now, with a simple implant and the right compression, in about five minutes you could get the full effect of as many hours of sleep as your budget allowed. With the advent of STATS, every business could run twenty-four hours a day and employees never missed their children's plays, going to the gym, grocery shopping, or watching HD3D for hours on end. Advertisers loved STATS. They get the same ad rates for 2:AM adverts as 8:PM. Viewer statistics never have a down time.

In the beginning, Sleepers were recruited. The government wanted the system to work, and there were more than enough people who thought sleeping most of the day would be the best job ever. Some even said the government put caffeine in the drinking water, so people would have to buy their sleep. Once the general population realized they could hook their STATS together and share sleep - without the government surcharges - the business went private.

Trading sleep didn't last long. People started by using it to catch up on lost hours, but after a while some went round-the-clock. The Rounders grew, till it was odd to find someone who still got by on their own sleep. Once nearly everyone went round-the-clock, you couldn't ask your friend for a couple hours. He wasn't sleeping either.

The average Joe on the street without a Corporate Sleeper went to a REM Shop. You could buy your five, six, even eight hours of sleep, for a nominal fee. Mobile phones came equipped with transfer STATS, standard. Sleep Shops sprung up for every application imaginable. The rich hired Personal Dreamers. Sleep was available for purchase in more locations than coffee. The only people missing out were the poor. They had to get by with actual sleep, sharing with friends who could still sleep, or Doze.

Doze is bottom of the rung sleep - No-REM. It isn't illegal, but a bit like eating from a trash can. Some sleeper who couldn't get a full night will go to a sleep shop and try to sell their hours, but the shops can tell the quality. If it doesn't compress well, they won't buy. It's the difference between regular coffee and decaf. Doze is decaf. It might give you a little boost, because it kind of feels like sleep, but your brain knows it's not real sleep. Even so, it can mean the difference between going without for a few days, or going without for a week. You can get by on Doze, maybe for long enough to score some real sleep. There's always some Sleep Merch who swears he bought pure sleep from a business source, but it's usually no-REM Doze.

Lucas called his friend Martin. Since Martin was liberated over a month ago and still hadn't found a chore, he was sure to have a sleep source. When Martin answered his phone, he sounded a little out-of-it. He told Lucas to meet him at Ashby and 3rd. At least, that's what Lucas could make out. It sounded like Martin was holding two conversations at once, and he was slurring his words. Ashby and 3rd was the only part Lucas caught that sounded like it was meant for him. He said six, but he didn't say AM or PM. No one gave a time without saying AM or PM. Military time never caught on. It was like trying to get everyone to switch to metric. Rounders knew you had to specify. Maybe Martin had been liberated too long.

Deciding AM, because it was only a few hours away, Lucas watched some HD3D to pass the time. National news said the stock market was down again. That was one of the reasons Lucas had been let go. The market neared a crash when everyone first went to no-sleep - too much production. After people realized how much time they had, consumption went back up and struck a balance. There are still dips though. A few competing companies will overproduce, till the government comes in and regulates.

Every fourth advert was for some type of sleep procurement option. Sleep Store America was offering a buy one week of sleep, get two days free sale. Buy forty weeks and get a whole year. Not a bad deal, if you can afford the forty weeks. There was an ad for a chore at Bronson Autocars. Lucas thought he'd stop by after he found Martin. Nothing was worse than showing up for a chore interview looking drowsy. Most businesses believed if you couldn't provide for your own sleep, you wouldn't be a good employee. If Duncan-Morse was even a little more sympathetic, they would have provided the liberated with a month's sleep credit. Lucas had heard some companies were adding it to their severance, but Duncan-Morse hadn't caught on yet.

Lucas splashed his face with water - nothing worse than looking sleep deprived in public - and headed to Ashby. Six AM looked a lot like any other time of the day - throngs headed to chores, Ed-Sys, shopping. This was an area of town Lucas rarely frequented. Rumors persisted that sleepers and STATS objectors made their homes here. Lucas looked around, but didn't see Martin. He leaned against a news box. The recording started.

"Current temperature, seventy-six. When will the new compressions protocols come into effect? Who was seen with Matt Crane at a private beach? Will ComTech buy Sysmet? Download your copy now. It's a twenty-four-hour world. World Global News can help you navigate it."

A man, attracted by the recording, approached the box. He was about Lucas' age, but fresh from his STATS charge, which made him look all of twenty-one. A good STATS charge can take five years off your face. The man jacked into the box with his phone and slipped his finger over the sensor, downloading his daily news. *"This man's fully charged, downloading news, headed to a chore, and here I am standing on the corner waiting for Doze. What has my life become?"* Lucas thought.

"Lucas, you know I hate this. Hey, Lucas. Stop calling me that."

Lucas turned to face Martin, but not the Martin he knew just a month ago. This man looked disheveled, hungry, tired.

"Martin? Man, it's been a while."

"I hate summer. Tuesday is worse. How you been, Lucas?"

"What? Fine. How are you doing?"

"Sick."

"I'm sorry to hear that."

"Tuesdays are sick and pink."

This was almost the same conversation Lucas had with Martin on the phone. He thought there was someone else in the room with him at the time, but standing here on the street, there was no one else.

"Martin, are you okay?"

"Oh, sure, Lucas. I never had cantaloupe. It's tasty, and I want a paper bag for now. You want to go somewhere and talk?"

With that last, barely comprehensible statement, Martin sank to the pavement like a deflated balloon. Lucas reached out to grab him, a second too late.

A few heads turned. Someone muttered, *'Crasher'*. A woman pulled her child off to the side and hurried past. Lucas gathered Martin up as best he could and tried to keep him up and move him down the street. He got him a block before he had to stop to rest, letting Martin's weight slide down to the pavement.

"I hope you Crashers get outlawed."

Lucas looked up. A man in a crisp chef's uniform rolled his eyes in disgust.

"He's sick," Lucas tried to explain.

"You're both sick." The chef stormed off.

"Martin?" A girl rushed up to Lucas and the slumped Martin. She knelt and cradled Martin's head in her hands.

"He just collapsed," Lucas explained.

"Marty, you'll be fine," she said, to the unconscious man at Lucas' feet. Then, she looked up. She wasn't bad looking, but the dark circles under her eyes meant she probably had no chore, and couldn't afford sleep. Her hair had been dyed with the wood-grain style that was so popular, but blond roots were showing, so it'd been a while since her last touch-up.

"Our place is about a block. Think you can get him that far?"

"I probably can."

"I got a wagon, if you want to wait with him."

"No, it's all right. Lead the way."

"Try putting him behind you with his arms over your shoulders. That way's usually best." She took the weight of the slumped Martin, while Lucas turned.

"Does this happen often? Is he sick?"

"He just went too long. He doesn't mean to crash, really. He's not a crasher. He couldn't score is all."

Lucas took her explanation, having no idea what a crasher was, or why it was important that he not think Martin was one.

They made their way to the girl's building. It was a small, slip of a doorway alongside an alley. Lucas glanced down the alley as the girl ran her finger over the security sensor. An unkempt teenager passed the other end, dragging a small wagon overflowing with another teen.

"I'm upstairs, first door on the left. Think you can make it?" she asked.

"I made it this far."

Lucas pulled Martin step by step, nearly losing his grip a few times, pushing himself so he wouldn't roll his friend down the stairs.

Inside the girl's apartment, she led Lucas to a room solely for sleeping. Lucas thought back to when he was a child and had one of these - a bedroom. It seemed like the most ridiculous waste of space to him now - a room set aside solely for sleeping - laying in this room, completely unconscious. People would decorate them and buy special furniture for them, and most of the time they were in them they weren't even aware of the room itself. Many had changed them into office/dressing areas. A few still had a bed for sexual encounters, but all new homes came with materooms; a smaller area off your dressing room, with a thick, cushioned floor. The materoom in his apartment had a food unit in the wall, and a music system. It was state of the art, heated cushions, rolling massage. Lucas realized it could just as easily be used for sleeping. Why hadn't he thought of that earlier? Maybe he could have logged some real sleep, and not ended up here.

"Sarah." The girl arranged Martin on the bed, pulling off his shoes.

"Lucas." He guessed that was her attempt at an introduction.

"I know. Martin told me he was going to meet you - either that or he was going to ride a potato chip to Mars." She laughed, and ruffled Martin's hair. Something in the way she looked down at Martin reminded Lucas of being a small boy and having his mother put him to bed. He felt a wave of drowsiness flood over him. It was warm and full, like a really good meal after a long day's work.

"He'll be fine in a few hours," Sarah said. She herded Lucas out of the room, and pulled the door shut quietly.

"Is he sick?"

"He just needs some sleep." She looked down, apparently embarrassed. "Want some tea?" She headed for the kitchen, quickly.

"Yes, that would be good." Lucas took a seat on the couch and looked around the room.

"Green or black?" Sarah called from the kitchen.

"Black, please."

The apartment was small, but very clean - freshly painted even. The coffee table was covered with books and magazines.

Sarah came in carrying two cups of tea. She set them on the table.

"I'm sorry, I forgot to ask, Sweetnet?"

"This is fine." Lucas picked up the cup and took a sip. It tasted bitter. She must have seen his expression.

"It's double-caf. It's all we have. Let me get you a little Sweetnet in it."

Lucas started to object, but she took the cup and walked back to the kitchen. Lucas looked around, glanced a few titles - Deprivation and You, How to Deprive, and Crasher's Guide. The latter looked like a self-published magazine. Lucas picked up the Crasher's Guide as Sarah came back in the room.

"That's not... its Blaze's. He left it here."

"Blaze?"

"He's a crasher. We're not crashers, really. Just because you can't afford to buy sleep, doesn't mean you're a crasher." She said it as though Lucas, himself, had called her that.

"Listen, I never even heard of Crashers, so you don't have to explain yourself to me."

"Sorry, people get the wrong impression. Poor is one thing... a crasher, that's a whole other thing all together."

Lucas nodded his head towards the bedroom. "So, he's really sleeping now?" Sarah nodded. "For how long?"

"He tells me to wake him after five hours, but I usually let him go up to nine."

"Nine hours?" Lucas was startled. The Martin he knew was a full-out Rounder - never slept a wink. How could he go from Rounder to Sleeper in a month?

"He's been seven days without."

"Is that the limit?"

"The longest he's gone is ten days. But, it's not like he does it on purpose."

"I didn't mean that." Lucas tried to explain. "I just... I got liberated two weeks ago. I tried sleeping, but I couldn't."

"No severance?"

"None. I borrowed from friends for a while. A couple hours here and there, but I don't want to overextend them. I didn't have any savings. I thought my job was secure. I can't afford the bills and sleep."

"How long have you been without?"

"Three days."

"Oh, you haven't even got to the good part yet."

"There's a good part?"

"No. I meant... so, why'd you call Martin?"

Lucas shifted a little in his seat. "I thought he might have a chore, or know of someone looking for workers."

"You're looking for Doze," Sarah smiled, and set her cup on the table. "We don't have any Doze."

"But, when I talked to Martin on the phone, he said he might..."

"We don't do that. Besides, when you talked to Martin, well... you saw what you were talking to. You go so long without and you start getting a little... crazy."

Martin leaned forward and put his cup on the table. "I'm sorry. I didn't have anyone else to call." He stood up.

"Which do you think is worse," Sarah asked. "A dozer, or a crasher?"

"I told you. I don't know what a crasher is."

Sarah reached over and picked up the Crasher's Guide. She handed it to Lucas.

"Read this and give us a call."

Lucas took the magazine and left.

It didn't take long for Lucas to get up to speed. Crashers held back sleep as long as they could, for the high. Then, they'd crash. When they awoke, they'd sell the sleep and start all over. Most people would only get a little disoriented, their speech would slur, and they'd pass out after a few days without. The ones who got hallucination, they were hooked.

The Crasher's Guide had hints and tips for keeping yourself up and going. A reader's area had personal accounts of visions and voices. Some seemed to think they could hear the voice of God, if they went long enough. The guide wasn't all bad. It had health tips for crashers and set the limit of days without at ten. There seemed to be an ongoing argument in the reader's area on whether two weeks really kills. There was even a website selling 'Two Weeks Kills' T-shirts.

The guide said Crasher sleep was high quality. Because of all the days without, a crasher usually had quality delta waves, which were ideal for compression. Some connoisseurs even sought out Crasher's sleep, solely.

From the look of Martin and Sarah's apartment, they didn't have the connections to sell the sleep. A lesser man would have seen this as an opportunity to get some prime sleep from an old friend. Lucas saw the start of his new chore.

World, Other World

As Strange As Most

The two Charlies saw the Orvand as soon as he came through the door. There wasn't a bartender in the known galaxies who didn't want to hide when an Orvand slumped into their joint.

"I saw him first, Two," Charlie One said, quickly.

"You did not. Your eye was on the Malgnar." The Malgnar looked up and smiled at the mention of his race. Charlie Two was already untying his apron. "I'm going on break."

Charlie One couldn't argue. He only had the one eye after all, dead center of the large lump that passed for a head, and he did have it trained on the Malgnar. You always have to have someone watching the Malgnar. They are known to reach over the bar, grab the vat of cherries for the fancy drinks, swallow them down - stems and all - in one gulp, then swear to Arthrah they saw someone else do it. Which is why the Malgnar's third arm is often called their 'cherry arm' in some parts of the galaxy. Charlie One only looked over to the door when he heard a small sigh from Charlie Two.

The Orvand made his way towards the bar through the crowd. Patrons parted to make way for him. It wasn't due to his size. Orvands only stand about five feet, maybe five six if they weren't so slumped, and barely weigh a hundred pounds. They have two small, useless wings high on each shoulder. Their appearance is not that unusual. No, what the patrons wanted to avoid was the Orvand addressing them. Once an Orvand starts talking, it takes little less than death - yours or theirs - to make them stop. If you walk away, they follow you. A bar is probably the best place to run into one. They don't hold their liquor very well. Once they pass-out, you're free to go.

A Sklurb, a bulbous creature from Delphi, tried desperately to get all his fifteen eyes to point in any direction save the Orvands, but one strayed, so he grabbed it and pulled it out. It's not as shocking as it sounds. It would grow back, eventually.

Charlie One, resigned to his fate, waited patiently for the Orvand to make its way to the bar. The Malgnar had left his stool by the cherry vat. In fact, all the stools had cleared, leaving poor Charlie One to face the Orvand alone.

"I've had a horrible day, Charlie." The Orvand dropped onto a stool. The greeting wasn't one of familiarity. All bartenders on spaceports go by the name, Charlie. It makes it easier and gives a sense of not being so far away from home.

"What can I get you?" Charlie One tried to sound cheerful, maybe a little busy.

"Just a Swish, if that's all right."

"Coming right up." Charlie One grabbed a glass and bottle. He filled the glass quickly and pushed it towards the Orvand.

"My planet is the worst planet in the known universe." That was the usual beginning to any Orvand conversation.

"Yes," Charlie One said, "I've heard it is."

This never worked. It didn't matter if you agreed with everything an Orvand said, even if you told them you've heard it all before. They still believed you needed to hear it one... more... time.

"We have dust storms that last a week. We had one just before I left."

Charlie One grabbed a bowl of mundles and a

knife. The vat was full, but he started slicing anyway. He knew this wouldn't work, either. Orvands never thought you were too busy to listen. They saw it more as their entertaining you while you work.

"Our young are born with claws two inches long. It takes three of us to clip them, and it's always hard to find a third."

Charlie One concentrated on the mundles.

"No one wants to be the third. Two of us hold the offspring, while the other has to bite off the claws."

The question of why one of the parents couldn't be the one to bite off the claws popped into Charlie One's head, but he quickly suppressed it. Though he knew it had never worked before, he was going to try to be as quiet as possible and hope to get the Orvand drunk enough to pass out.

"See this scar?" The Orvand pointed to a long gash on the side of his neck. "First born. And this one, second born." On through to his ninth born, the Orvand pointed out his scars. If it were possible, the Orvand seemed to slouch even more than usual. "My tenth is due any day now."

Charlie One thought he heard the door to the back open and swung around to have a look. The door stood silent.

"Did you ever hear about the trees on Pradux?" the Orvand started.

"Yeah, they roam about eating the crops," Charlie One volunteered, despite his best intentions.

"And there's no stopping them. They drink pesticides like... well, Swish."

"Speaking of which, can I get you another?"

"I want to go slow tonight. Thanks. I've had a bad day." The Orvand slurped a small, loud sip from his glass. "I'm heading back to Pradux tomorrow. It's Crouse Season. Heard of it?" Charlie One knew a response wasn't necessary.

"The crouse are our main source of food, but they sting like the fires of Selgoron when you pick them up."

"Couldn't you skewer them, then kill them?" Like many failed Charlies before him, Charlie One could not overcome the desire to reply. Some theorized the Orvand's had a gift for getting people to respond. The Federation had tried using them as interrogators, hoping the natural tendency of most races to interact with them would lead to confessions. Instead, they ended up with tapes and tapes of Orvands telling suspects about the horrible conditions on their home planet, Pradux. A few confessed, just to get away from the Orvands, but the confessions wouldn't hold up. Anyone would sympathize with the plight of the suspect. Some claimed cruel and unusual punishment.

"We eat them live." The Orvand was still going on about the crouse. "Have to catch them, then bring them home and care for them. A dead crouse is thin as a leaf. All the spirit goes out of it, so there's no nourishment. We have crouse pens. At meals we put on our special lip covers, grab one and suck the spirit out. It's a little bitter, but it's all we have - what with the trees eating the crops."

A Freen sidled up to the bar. Sightless, but with a fair sense of smell, he caught the essence of Orvand as he reached his paw onto the counter. His fluffy down covering changed from a bright pink - a sign of happiness - to dark blue.

"Kartoosh?" Charlie One grabbed the bottle and slid it into the Freen's outstretched paw. The Freen snatched it and wobbled quickly off.

"We tried making gloves of the same material as our lip covers, but they gave us all a rash."

"That's a shame." Charlie One trailed off on the word shame. He knew better. Orvands live for sympathy. They relish it like Malgnars relish cherries. "Another Swish?"

"I guess so." The Orvand sounded almost pleased. He seemed to sit a little taller. He had found a sympathetic ear.

Charlie One poured the Swish and set it on the counter.

"You know what? We have one day of darkness for every three days of light. That doesn't seem fair, does it?"

The door to the back room creaked open. Charlie One turned to see Charlie Two coming out. He was tying on his apron, a piece of paper clasped between his teeth as he made the knot. Charlie One gave him a desperate look. Charlie Two winked at him. Charlie One had learned this was actually a playful gesture, not an attempt to brag that he had two eyes, but it still seemed inappropriate given his current situation.

Charlie One looked out at the crowd. There was a small group standing off to the side, waiting for Charlie, any Charlie, to refill their drinks. Instead of tending to them, Charlie Two walked right over to Charlie One and the Orvand and set his sheet of paper in front of him.

"I got this," he told Charlie One.

"Our lips are a different material than our hands," the Orvand was saying, holding out his hands to show them. "So the gloves simply wouldn't work."

Charlie One didn't stop to ask why Charlie Two was willing to take on the Orvand. He slipped to the end of the bar to help those waiting for their drinks.

"You got it pretty bad on Pradux, huh?" Charlie Two asked.

"Sure do, Charlie. Like I was telling Charlie, we only have three days of sunlight to every day of night."

"Really? That's a shame. Crying shame," Charlie Two told him. This got Charlie One's attention. No one purposely supports an Orvand's believed strife. "I know a place," Charlie Two started, "with only two-thirds of a day in light, and one third in darkness."

"But," the Orvand said, "they probably have better night vision than we do."

"They don't have any night vision. Not any worth mentioning at least."

"So, they do have some then? And what about their foods. Our main food..." Charlie Two interrupted the Orvand. "They have food with claws that can pinch you, and food that if not cooked properly will kill them, and insects that eat their food, and animals that eat their food..."

"But, they have food. Sometimes the crouse run out. We have to live on what little crops the trees haven't found. Do they have trees like ours?"

"You have me there. Their trees aren't small and

roaming. They're stationary, but sometimes six or more times taller than they are, and high winds make them fall. In the cold season, the trees hibernate, so they provide no protection."

"Do you know about our lakes? They sometimes run dry," the Orvand countered.

"They have tons of water. More water than dry land." Charlie Two leaned on the bar facing the Orvand. A small hush went over the crowd. Charlie Two looked up. The patrons had gathered near the end of the bar, in awe of someone purposely coaxing an Orvand on.

"Last year, after the dust storm, our lakes were almost dry. Our wells would only last a season. We didn't know if the rainy season would come on time or not."

"But see, they have all this water all over their planet, but they can't drink most of it. It would kill them. Surrounded by water, yet they're unable to drink it."

The Orvand fell silent for a second. He took a long slurp of his Swish. Charlie Two filled his glass without asking.

"They have insects that feed on them constantly - small ones, flying ones. They have insects that can kill them with a single bite."

"We have Tongas. Tongas are small creatures who try to tear off our wings - useless as they are."

"They have large beasts on land and in the water that can eat them in a second." Charlie Two snapped his fingers, startling the Orvand, who gathered himself with another slurp of his drink. "They have plants that, not only can't they eat them, they can't touch them, not even brush up against them without getting a horrible, itchy, oozing rash." Someone in the crowd gasped.

"Our planet's orbit makes us spend only three quarters of our year in the warmth of our sun, and the rest in the cold."

"Their atmosphere allows in dangerous light from their sun. It can burn their skin, their eyes, it can blind them if they look directly at it. Some parts are constantly frozen, some are periodically so hot they can barely breathe."

The Orvand slurped his Swish down, and Charlie Two refilled it again without asking.

"Throughout their year they spend most of their time in buildings with artificial atmospheres. They have to, because the temperature outside their buildings is too cold or too hot to survive."

"Balderdash!" the Orvand exclaimed, or that is the best translation. No one had ever heard the word this Orvand shouted, and they could only guess at its meaning in retrospect.

"Winds and storms bring down their homes, send electricity sometimes striking them or their buildings - starting fires. Storms lash the water up onto their land bringing down their buildings." Charlie Two stared intently at the Orvand.

Perhaps, if Orvands had some sense of humour, he would have laughed it off. As it was, the Orvand stared back for what seemed a full minute. Then, he picked up his glass and swallowed the last of his Swish. He set the glass loudly on the counter, got up, and headed for the door.

The patrons in the bar stood silent, watching the Orvand make his slow, silent exit. As the door closed behind him, an enthusiastic murmur rose from the crowd. They gathered at the bar in excited chatter, holding out their glasses for Charlie Two to fill and dropping more coins in his tip jar than he would usually get in a week.

"That was some tall tale." Charlie One slapped Charlie Two on the back. "You almost had me believing it."

"All true," Charlie replied, shaking a paw extended by a customer in congratulations. "I've told you about Earth before - maybe not so much about those things. All in all, makes me a little homesick."

World, Other World

What if We Lose Saturday?

Reuben got out of his car at the corner of Fifth and Wilson, following the readout on his locator. He stopped and looked down the block. He had expected a crowd, but there was only a steady stream of people heading to work.

"I am Will Johnson. I am your governor." Reuben heard a small voice up ahead, slightly hoarse and halfhearted. No one seemed to notice. Slipping through the crowd, he made his way towards the voice.

Halfway down the block, beside a news box, stood William H. Johnson. He was dressed in a fine Italian suit, his briefcase on the ground beside him. Johnson's hand was out, business card extended to anyone who'd take it, but most averted his gaze.

"I am Will Johnson. I am your governor," he

repeated.

"Tom Peterson's the governor. You're just some bum in a business suit." An angry man swatted Johnson's extended hand from his path.

Reuben tapped a few buttons on his locator and whispered 'I have him' into his mouthpiece. He slipped the locator into his pocket and walked up to Johnson.

"Mr. Johnson?"

Johnson looked up with a smile, hoping he was finally getting someone's attention. The smile slipped from his face immediately, and he twitched as though he might run. Reuben touched his arm lightly.

"Let's do this nicely, okay?"

"I'll tell them about the waves. I'll tell everyone."

"They won't believe you." Reuben put his hand on Johnson's shoulder and turned him towards the waiting car.

"I won't accept this." There was no conviction in his voice.

"You knew the risk."

Reuben brought Johnson back to PIM headquarters and turned him over to the Assimilation Team. Many top psychiatrists and social engineers from throughout the world worked for Parallel Interference Management. Johnson would be an easy case. He already knew what had happened. His government status had given him access to mag-field stasis. It wasn't mandatory stasis, as was the case with higher levels of government, but the option was there. Lower-level officials were warned against using the option, but the risks were so small, few paid any heed.

Reuben lost his wife in the first wave. More accurately, the first wave he realized. He was at the hospital getting an MRI when it hit. He didn't know it happened, but when he returned home, the house where he lived wasn't his anymore. A strange woman answered the door, after his key wouldn't work. He summoned police, sure it was all an elaborate practical joke. They asked if he had been drinking. When he told them his story, they treated him like a mental patient. He pulled out his driver's license to prove his point, only to find a different address. His wallet no longer contained the picture of his wife. The police were ready to take him in when a stranger walked up, claiming to know him. In his confused state, he took the man's word for it and agreed to go with him. That was his first trip to PIM headquarters.

The psychiatrist assigned to him was supposed to use hypnosis to clear his memory, reset the circumstances of his life to the current situation, but Reuben wouldn't go under. They called in others, with the same results. Rather than fight him, they sat him down and explained the predicament.

He had a fragmented understanding of physics, but was familiar with the concept of parallel dimensions, mostly from movies and television. They explained simply.

Parallel dimensions were bumping against each other, causing slight changes in the realities of the worlds with every encounter. He never married his wife. Perhaps, they never even met. It may have been the MRI that blocked him from the wave. Most people never knew anything was different. Life as it was, was life as it always had been, even if major changes had taken place.

There were always a few strays - people who turned on the news to find Alaska was now part of the United States. Most wrote it off to their own ill-attention. Some tried to convince others that something was different or wrong and wound up in a mental hospital or at PIM headquarters. Reuben convinced them he could accept the circumstances, though only vaguely grasping what it all meant.

Rather than move on with his life in its current state, Reuben set out to meet, or re-meet, his wife. When he finally found her, she was married with four children and living a state away. He talked to her only once, in a grocery store. He hoped there might be some small glimmer of recognition when he approached, but he found nothing in her eyes.

"Excuse me. Have we met before?" he said.

She said she didn't recall. Reuben brought up the movie where they'd met. Her children tugged at her, and the baby in her arms started to cry.

"Hush now, will you?" She turned back to Reuben and said she wished she could find a sitter. Her hair, her eyes, they were all strong in his memory, but it was like looking at her twin. The features were the same, but she was not the woman he'd married.

Reuben scoured the news for months after his encounter with the interference wave. Nowhere was there any mention of problems with parallel universes. There were physics papers dealing with string theory and the existence of parallel dimensions, but nothing about an ongoing situation. He eventually came across a website called Wave Jumpers. The author rambled on about the interference waves and the site had layouts and blueprints for building a device that would block the wave interference. Reuben clicked through to a few sites, checking the cost of the equipment. An hour later, there was a knock at his door. That was his second trip to PIM headquarters.

Reuben was brought into Commander Ted Swift's office and asked to take a seat. Ten minutes later, a tall, distinguished man came through the door.

"Reuben Groule?" He put out his hand. Reuben stood, nodding and shook his hand. "Sit. Make yourself comfortable. Sorry for the delay."

Reuben sat down. Swift made his way around the desk.

"Notice anything strange while you waited?"

Reuben was taken aback by the question. He thought, perhaps, a wave had come through while he had sat in the chair, unknowing.

"Did I? Did we just... get hit?"

Swift laughed. "No, I thought you might have had a chance to look around a bit."

Reuben glanced quickly around the room. Something caught his eye. He looked over at Swift, then back to a poster for a movie named Caliber.

"That's one," Swift said. "Best damn John Wayne movie ever. Not that anyone knows that anymore. Good thing I hung on to the poster, right?"

"How can a movie disappear?"

"It didn't disappear. It was never written. Wish I

had a DVD at the office, too. All I have left is that poster and my memory." Swift stared up at the poster with a glimmer in his eye. "What the hell. Maybe, I'll write the thing up myself and sell it to Hollywood."

"Yes, sir."

"Sir isn't necessary. Relax, Groule."

"It's just... I don't know why I'm here."

"You aren't in any trouble. Don't worry about that. We don't pull in everyone who visits the jumper sites. But, since we had a file on you - the two together... well, we wanted to check it out."

"That gum." Reuben leaned forward and pointed to a pack on Swift's desk, "That's different." He looked around a bit more. "And the dog in the photo with you. I'm sure I've never seen that breed."

"Metahaunee. Originally a rodent hunter in Hawaii. I sure miss her." Swift picked up the picture and smiled. "They're working on this one. I might get another, one day."

"They, sir?"

"Swift. Just call me Swift. We're not that formal around here." He set the photo down. "*They*, is a long story. You have a good eye, and I read your background." Swift opened a folder on his desk. "Corporate trainer. No

135

criminal record. Sorry about the wife."

Reuben nodded. "May I ask what all this is about?"

"We could use a fellow like you around here."

"To do what, sir... Swift?"

"Clean up."

Swift took Reuben through the compound. The entire building was wired to emit an electromagnetic field, stabilizing it when an interference wave hit. Several offices had dog and cat kennels off to the corner. The chances of losing a pet were about one in a trillion, trillion, or some equally incomprehensible number Swift explained, but it seemed many were unwilling to accept those odds. Swift blamed his own loss for the others' concern.

The detection system relied on sensors. Sensors had been up and running for four years, perfected to sense an interference wave over a blip in the field, but a device to predict the waves was still in its infancy. Large changes in the Earth's EMF would trigger an alarm. Workers, scientists and their families could all gather within the compound to ride the wave. A wave only lasted a millisecond, but everyone would have to stay inside until the reports came in. Minor political changes could cause problems, but those were usually found right away. The full reports could take days to find every change.

"We've averaged only one major change per year - things like Castro, he died in the eighties - but the minor changes run about ten to twenty per wave. Things as small as the penny - it used to have Taft on it. They did a survey on that one. No one was willing to give up Abraham. Tax day changed from the thirteenth of March. I think everyone was pleased with that."

Governments in the US and foreign countries all had their own compounds. An international group of PIM members dealt with the changes, deciding a course of action for major events took three quarters agreement. Going against PIM could mean destruction of your country's compound. Laboratories were set aside. Redevelopment was an international endeavor.

"Some of the best scientists in the world now work for us," Swift explained. "All their previous work, their status, their funding, could all be wiped out with one wave that they wouldn't even know happened. It wasn't hard to convince them."

With the laboratories, the diplomats, PIM was like a small country unto itself, outside the normal operation of the world. Its only contacts with the general population were the clean up crews. This was the job Swift was offering Reuben.

"It can be hard work, or it can be easy. With your training abilities, you'd fit right in."

"What would it entail?"

"There's not too much that falls on the crews' shoulders. Most people, the general population, they don't even know what's going on. One second a guy works for Capitol Income and the next he's bagging groceries. But, bagging groceries is all he remembers, so it's all right." Swift shrugged. "But, every wave there are a few people who don't seem to get hit. Things change, but they see the change.

"Then, there are the jumpers. We try to catch them, but the smarter we get, the smarter they get. Most end up in mental facilities. Who's going to care if Sam's Burgers was always known to have a blue building, but now it's pink? They start screaming about a colour change and they're either ignored or someone decides they need some mental help."

"So, the guy on the street corner telling me... I don't know... cars used to fly?"

"Yeah, only they didn't fly. Not since I started. We were lucky to get hybrids a few years ago in a wave. The technology we had at the time was no where near ready."

Reuben signed on that day. His motivation was knowing he would always remember. Sometimes late at night he wondered which was better, the knowing or the not knowing.

After dropping off Governor Johnson, Reuben headed to Swift's office. The watch commander was running over the interference report. Reuben stopped at the door and knocked lightly.

"Good job, Groule." Swift's gaze stayed on his screen. "He give you any trouble?"

"Not a bit. He was already talking about running again on the ride down here."

Swift motioned for Reuben to have a seat.

"Anything major pop up?" he asked, dropping into the chair opposite the desk.

"Nope." Swift finally looked up from his screen. "We lost some ant. Nothing I ever heard of, and the entomologist on staff can't find any repercussions, so we should be okay with that. Not that there's a thing we could do about it. It's not in the DNA database."

"Any luck pinning down a pattern?" Reuben asked.

"They thought they had it worked out, but this last one was completely outside the equations. The fields are good now, and we don't see readings for anything soon. All the sensors are blue. Could be a two-day window. Could be a month."

"I'm going home to get some sleep then, if that's all right."

"Sure. We go yellow, I know where to reach you."

Reuben stood up to leave.

"How far along are they with the beer?"

"You don't like sake?" Swift tapped the bottle sitting on his desk. The label read: 'Wild Bill's Cranberry Sake'.

"I had it once, years ago, didn't like it."

"It's not the same sake we had. They have hundreds of variations."

"You mean, 'we have'. This is our world now."

"We. They." Swift shrugged. "They'll probably reintroduce a beer variation in about two weeks, but you know protocol. The German PIM members have first rights to the lager. There are about three countries still arguing over ale."

Reuben sighed. He'd spent the day running around cleaning up all the loose ends from the interference wave, and tonight there was no cold beer anywhere in the world.

"Go down to the lab. They've been working on

formulas all day," Swift told him. "They could probably use another test subject."

Reuben came home to an empty apartment carrying a thermos of beer the lab techs were kind enough to give him. It didn't taste like his regular brand, but nothing probably ever would. He sat down at his computer and ran his routine search for his name and the word 'sandwich' - the same hits as usual.

One day he was hoping to find his namesake. It was lost before he joined PIM, before PIM was even set up, so no one knew exactly what it was. He only knew there was a sandwich with his name, because a wave-jumper mentioned it. The man was disheveled and barely comprehensible, but he had greeted Reuben with the comment, "Like the sandwich?"

Reuben questioned him about it, but the man couldn't remember too much, and what he did say didn't make much sense - something about sauerkraut and salad dressing. It didn't sound appetizing, but every time a wave came through Reuben checked to see if it was back. For almost a year July had gone back to the original name of Quintilis, so there was always a chance of it returning, though he knew the odds were slim.

World, Other World

It Was a Gesture

I'm not normally a helpful person. I have helped people before, don't get me wrong, but I don't go out of my way. It's my philosophy that you shouldn't help anyone who's more than capable of helping himself and just doesn't want to do it. That philosophy has gotten me through life with little need to lend an extra hand. I have to rethink that philosophy, as soon as I get home. I don't know when that will be. I'm not even sure why I'm fighting. All I know is right now I'm lying in a trench, God only knows where, and these creatures keep coming at us. Every few minutes someone yells *'Go'*, and I have to rise up and hit this little blue button on this massive piece of plastic I'm holding as many times as I can in the few seconds that follow. Then, someone yells *'Stop'*.

This all started about a week ago, according to the

days on my watch. If I didn't have the watch, I would have guessed it was months ago, or even a lifetime ago, but according to the watch, it's only been a week.

Maybe I was feeling generous that day. It was the start of the week. So, maybe coming off the weekend, I was in a better mood. I really can't explain why it happened, even though it was only a few days ago. My watch says it's Saturday. I should be at home now, mowing the lawn, or watching a movie on TV. Instead, I'm in this ditch. But I'm getting sidetracked. I want to tell you how I got here, as best I can remember.

Monday seems like a good place to start. I was on my way into the building where I work. It was a beautiful day. The kind of day that makes you want to play hooky. I was coming out of the parking deck when Harvey, one of the company heads, walked up.

"Have you seen Richard?" He had a worried look on his face.

"No, I just got here."

"He was supposed to get here early to run some designs down to the south office." That explained the portfolio. Harvey rarely had anything but a cup of coffee in his hand.

"I'm sure he's only running late." Now, you have to understand; Harvey is one of the big bosses. He's an

144

exception to my rule. Sure, he can help himself, but you know how it is with work hierarchy. So I added, "If there's anything I can do?" - just like that, like a question. It was a leading question, but like I said, he's a big boss.

"Would you mind?" That was all he said. He held out the portfolio. I took it, and he walked away, simple as that. I already said it was the perfect day to play hooky, so you have to understand. It was a single offer, to a single man, for a single task - that's it.

I made all the lights going down to the south office, so I decided to take the long way back. I had the windows down and the sun-roof open. My tie was lying on the seat beside me. It was great. Then, I see this lady on the side of the road.

I had to pull over. I mean, really. My luck was going well, getting to play hooky, at least for a little while, and making all the lights. She was wearing a dress and the hood was up on the car, so you could tell she wasn't going to fix it herself. Plus, she probably had a cell phone. The tow truck was probably already on the way. All I was going to do was pull alongside her car and ask if she needed help. A bit of karmic insurance is all.

Turns out she did have a cell phone. She tells me a tow truck is on the way, but she can't reach her husband, and the tow driver can't drop her off. She was just about to call a taxi, but if I could drop her off a few miles down the road? She needs to see her sister off for the airport. The sister, no answer on her phone either. I could have told her I would be late for work. I could have, but I didn't. I knew the area she was headed, and it really wasn't out of my way, so I told her to get in.

It was a short drive, and she made nervous conversation the whole way. I guess she was afraid I was some serial killer. She should have been able to tell by looking at me; I couldn't hurt a fly. Normally, that is. I am killing these creatures every time they yell *'Go'*, but this is different.

I almost had a look at one of the things when it got past the guy next to me. It looked like a pig or a warthog, but running on its hind legs. I could have gotten a better look, but I had to shoot the thing. Speaking of the guy next to me, he's from Brooklyn. Can you believe it? He's not sure how he got here either, but Brooklyn and Chicago are miles apart. Also, he's not so good a shot, but that's okay. I'm getting better by the minute, and I take up the slack. But, let me get back to my story.

After I dropped her off, I decided to head back to work post haste. I got to my office and was about to go through the mail, when my boss came in. I don't see my boss very often. I see Harvey, because he's always in the break room, but my own boss hides in his office all day - maybe trying to keep out of Harvey's way.

"Heard you gave Harvey a hand this morning?" He didn't even look at me when he talked. Maybe he's just the shy type.

"Yes sir."

"Think you could help me out? I need someone to fly into Pennsylvania to calm a client. Not as hard as it sounds. They just want to see a company representative with the contract."

"When would I leave?"

"This evening. You should be back tomorrow night."

Yes, I agreed to do it. It was a standard contract. My office had written it up, so I could carry it off. Plus, it was like a little break and added faith from my boss.

If you're thinking I could have said no, maybe you never worked for a big organization. Maybe you were never the little guy, who had to make some concessions to get ahead. You can't tell your boss 'No'. Some things are easier to do, than to not do. This was one of them.

I don't remember too much about Philadelphia. I was a little woozy that night, after dinner and drinks with the client. Turned out to be a great fellow, who just seemed a little lonely for company. I think he would have signed the contract even if my boss didn't send someone along.

The next day, I got up and packed my stuff back up. I remember putting everything in the one suitcase, but for some reason I now have my suitcase and a black sack by my cot in the building where they keep us. The sack isn't mine, but we decided if no one claims it by tonight we'll open it.

The guy from Brooklyn has his stuff with him to, but last he remembers he was headed to a soccer game, so none of his stuff is of much use to us out here. We drank all the beer in his cooler the first day. It's dry out here, like a desert, but dark most of the time. We finished off his chips earlier today. They give us some kind of army-style food packs. The chips are the closest we've had to real food

since we got here, so we rationed them - as much as we could. See, we've been here about four days - according to my watch, that is.

Where was I? Oh yeah, Philadelphia. So, I packed my stuff and headed to the airport. I made it back to Chicago. I remember that. Then, when I was walking through the airport, I bumped into this fellow. He was taller than me and built pretty solid, but when I bumped him he turned around with a really scared look on his face.

"Sorry," I said.

"No, it's okay." He looked down at my bag. "Coming or going?"

"Just got back from Philadelphia," I told him.

Brooklyn, the guy next to me, he bumped into someone too, in a parking lot. I think that might be how this happened. The guy in Chicago, he started talking about my work and all. I remember at one point he said he wanted to go to the men's room, but he was afraid to leave his bag. I'm really not a helpful guy, really I'm not, but I told him I'd watch it for him. He had a big blue sticker on his jacket. It was kind of holographic and looked like a company logo. I noticed he had one just like it on his bag. They're on everything here, even this piece of plastic I'm shooting. Well, he peels the sticker off his jacket and slaps it on my back.

"So I can spot you when I come out," he said. He started to walk away, but stopped. Reaching in his jacket, he pulled out another sticker and slapped it on my overnight bag. "You might need that."

At the time, I thought he meant, *'I might need that'*. Like, in case he didn't see the one on my back, but now I don't think that's what he meant at all. Still, was kind of nice of him. I let Brooklyn use my razor yesterday. He's still trying to find out how to get a toothbrush.

Well, that's how I got here. At least, that's the last thing I remember. Maybe someone asked me to lend them a hand. Maybe they asked if I could help them out. I don't usually help people; honest I don't. I know they handed me this weapon, pointed to the blue button, and said, *"When you hear 'Go', shoot. When you hear 'Stop' stop."* So that's what I'm doing.

The New World

Still the rains came. Renya could barely remember the time without the rains. Could it have really been only a few weeks? The tiles of the exedra where cold on her warm feet. She walked, with her now cooling cup of coffee, across the room for what seemed the hundredth time. Again, with no purpose.

She entered the dining area and set her coffee on the warmer for just a moment. *"Perhaps that's what brought me here?"* she thought. She glanced at the window as a lightning bolt lit up the sky, then retrieved her now steaming cup. The rain echoed outside as she sipped. It lightly tapped the stone walls of her home and streamed down the crystal windows surrounding the exedra. Every few minutes the light of the storm would flash through the windows, illuminating the white tiles of the floor with the glowing colours of the crystals.

Renya found the first weeks of the stormy season

the hardest. The desire to go outside was still fresh in her mind. She had read a little, listened to music discs, anything to pass the time. Renya lived in the area for three years. She had seen three stormy seasons and during each had decided not to stay another year, but move further inland. Every year, at the start of the rainy season, she changed her mind. A few days more and the thought of being inside for so long would sink in, then she would get down to work. The metal objects she'd found after last years rains would be a sculpture by the end of this rainy season. She had already titled it Independence, though the form was still vague in her mind. She was looking forward to the storm's end, so she could go out to the flat lands at the back of her home and see what the winds and waves had brought in from the other time.

Renya was born somewhere far east of here, but since the plague the world had changed so much. Over two-thirds of the planet's population was gone. No one was sure how it began. When Renya asked her father about the start of the plague, he told her they'd get to the bottom of it, but the bottom was simply too far down.

The world was a much different place now than what she read in the few books still left. Most of the books about the world's history were newer. They told of an old world that was a very unorganized place. People of different likes scattered about the planet. Renya had only been two when the others died. Her father had survived the plague and now lived in the Techforward community on the Eastland, as an elder physicist. There were some yet alive who were in their higher years, some as old as fifty-five, but mostly the children were immune. The planet's average age was now around twenty-five. Renya was twenty-two.

Starting at ten, Renya had spent her required two years in the varied communities that now existed on each continent. This community of art on Westland was where she felt she belonged. Art communities were one of the few places that allowed you to look back and forward. It offered the most freedom of all the communities. The science communities - Airforward, Medforward, Techforward, Telforward, ...forward, forward, forward... all those communities claimed the old world was a stagnant, nostalgic place; a place where people could not advance because they had not accepted how far they had gone and held too long on old ideals. When the new, younger minds took over, advances were quickly made. They reevaluated technologies that were overlooked or dismissed by the other generations.

All the scientists gathered to share knowledge, and with the help of those in the arts, developed a plan for communities to be set up around the planet. With minimal population, people migrated towards each other, and better climates. The Beltlands was the chosen name.

It took in lands encircling the planet - areas most habitable, and comfortable.

The children, as that was what most of the population was at the time, were sent among the communities. Adults relocated around the Beltlands, forming living and learning communities. There, they cared for the children. There was no true governing power, but a head of each sector. The sector leaders made up the Council of the Beltlands. Most communities were for technical training, a few were culturelands, but there was only one sector for arts.

Culturelands were the most fun for Renya. In the culturelands you could learn of the people who had once inhabited the area. They were not part of the Forward communities. Renya had stayed for a year with a dark-skinned family in Chinaland. They wore the dress of the culture, as did Renya during her stay, though it was not their native land. The long robes and wide pointed hats helped protect their tight-curled hair and dark skin from the sun.

Renya walked across the room to the sound system and put in a disc. The discs from before sang of love, death, fighting and copulation. Some of the old music was coarse and made her anxious. This disc was one of her favorites. To her, it sounded like a friend, sitting with her, and talking of life before the plague. It used similes and metaphors instead of blatant statements. A woman was a rose; this was a beautiful picture to her. The singer had a slight twang in his voice. The cover only said Williams, as artist images were not allowed. She imagined him tall, with long brown hair and deep brown eyes. Perhaps he was wearing a skirt of animal skins she had seen or, she supposed, he could have dressed like her and many others of this community, in loose comfortable pants and soft flowing shirts. She chose to imagine him in the skirt. He seemed too earthy to wear the cotton tunics now available, even as comfortable as they were.

Renya sipped her coffee and watched a stream of light dance across the floor. There were no meetings in the town hall during stormy season. An occasional Cynet meeting, but she wouldn't have to log on if she didn't want to. It would be six to eight weeks in the house alone. A friend had invited her to stay with him, but she felt she could use the time alone. If it was an emergency, she could telecom someone. Only the community meds ventured out in the storms. If she wanted someone to talk to, they were only a call away, but right now she just wanted to watch the rain.

Renya moved her chair over to the window. All the Cali Desert would be covered by now. She looked out of the window and at the window almost simultaneously. In the past three years she had collected remnants from the bygone era before the plague, after the land west of her current home had sunk into the ocean, only to slowly rise each year as the water from the storms recede. Many of the objects washed ashore after the rains were unfamiliar to her.

After the skies cleared, there was always a meeting in the town hall and members from the coast of the commune brought the strangest of the found items for others to see. It was like a game, trying to figure out what the objects had once been. Many found items were pieces of the past era's technologies. The current Forward leaders had done away with all the older appliances. With most of the population gone, there had been more than enough of the latest products for everyone. A case of large, black, vinyl discs was found the year before last. The grooves showed that information had been entered onto them, but no one could find anything to release the information.

Renya's friend Christopher had found the discs. When all hope was given up of getting the information from them, he tiled his dining area floor with them and covered it with a sheet of poly shipped from New Virginia. Last year someone found a description of a thing called a phonograph and asked Christopher, if they made one, would he dismantle his floor so they could try it. Luckily, Christopher had two or three discs left over. Since every disc was alike he didn't have to take his floor apart, but the guy who wanted to build the phonograph was having trouble making the parts. The information he found was vague at best and the Forward leaders did not like people delving into the past. *"Perhaps,"* Renya thought, *"he'll finish by the end of this season."*

Renya wondered what the Forward community would think of them making a phonograph. No cultural items from the middle of the twentieth century to the plague were even in the museums. The Forward leaders called it the 'Dead Century'. Renya was taught that by the end of the 1900's everything but science had become nostalgic. All the art, music and fashions were redone, decade by decade. Culture had stalled. Lacking new ideas, old ideas from a decade or two past were simply redressed, though sometimes renamed. To start anew, the elders had chosen old culture and the newest in technology only.

The music discs were the only traces of the time right before the plague. Though the Forward communities had done their best to discourage music from the dead century, the only format that survived through the plague panic were the discs, and some held very old music, preformed by twentieth century musicians. Rather than sort through them all, they agreed to release them into the public. The discs had performers' names and song titles on them, some had the lyrics with them, but all the covers were the same - just white paper with the performers' name. Many people, especially in this community, had drawn on the disc packaging, pictures of what they thought the performers looked like, or what they thought the songs were about, or their own picture in case someone borrowed their disc. Renya put swatches of cloth beneath the plastic on her discs. She used the colour and texture of the cloth to show the mood of the music. It made it easy to pick a disc without having to remember the performer's names. Moreover, she enjoyed picking the cloth when a new disc came in.

Christopher had made Renya a custom disc and gave it to her the day he left the Cultureland. The disc contained songs he believed were of a spiritual nature. Little of that type of music survived. The Forward leaders said it was because the people who believed in God were primitive and thought the plague was their God turning His back on them, so they destroyed their songs to Him. Christopher found spiritual meaning in many songs, and the disc of hymns he gave her only made her more curious about this belief in a higher being. Her favourites were by an artist named Sweet Matthew. His song Nothing Lasts reminded her of the plague, sadly, but sweetly. Divine Intervention was Christopher's inspiration to move on from the Cultureland. He had set off a few days before the rainy season began.

Though he told the community leaders he was taking a trip to Euroland, he was headed for a continent he had only heard of in whispered rumor. The island was said to be in Oceania, but none of the maps showed a large land mass in that area. Christopher had met a man named Val who claimed his ancestors came from a vast continent in the Pacific Ocean. He told him many refused to leave the land when the Beltlands communities were formed. It was not against laws to live in places other than the Beltlands. It was only considered counter to the good of the remaining population. There were a few beyonders who lived outside the Beltlands and in the last ten years, with the population growing, the Beltlands themselves had expanded north and south. With no map or globe showing an island in the area, Renya believed it must have been more than a group of beyonders - if the island did exist.

The Cynet system beeped, startling Renya back to the present. She walked over to her console and awakened the screen. Tyrell's image appeared.

"Did I wake you, Renya?"

"No. Just watching the rains."

"I don't know how you can live so close to the waters."

"How else can I get to everything that washes ashore before you and Dana? Is there anything wrong?"

"Everything is right. Dana delivered! It's a boy! He has the antibody for the plague."

"Congratulations! What are you naming him?"

"Dana insisted on Siberus - for her other land. She wants to teach him about the land where she was born. I don't even know if I'm pronouncing it properly." Tyrell turned to the look off to the side.

Renya heard Dana in the background. "Yes. Siberus. Tell her he's beautiful." Tyrell looked back at his screen.

"Did you hear that?" Renya nodded. "You'll have to come see him when the rains stop. Dana will call tomorrow, then you can at least see him on screen. Dana won't go in front of the monitor right now. She says she's a mess."

Dana called out, "I am, and I'm not letting him go, not for a second."

"I have others to call," Tyrell said.

"Give Dana my love." Tyrell nodded off to the side.

"She says the same. Take care." The screen went back to the Cynet menu. The incoming call icon blinked. Renya clicked it. Christopher appeared on the screen.

"Renya! Hey!"

"Christopher! Where are you?"

"I found it. I found the island!" Christopher's eyes were wide. He looked like he hadn't slept in a few days.

"So quickly? It really exists? What is it? Who lives there?" The questions rolled out of her.

"It's called... Australia. You have to come here."

"It's the rainy season. I can't leave."

"As soon as the rains end, then. You won't believe it. They have artifacts they use every day. I found a phonograph the first day I was here."

"A working one?" It had taken them months to even find out what played the vinyl discs Christopher had found.

"Working. All relics working. It's like going back into the time before the plague. Renya, they have churches here. Honest to goodness churches! They have music, history, government unlike anything we were taught. That's why they were removed from the maps."

"Is it safe there?"

"It is, but this connection is illegal. They aren't allowed Cynet access. I made a packet of information, in case we get cut off. Open the attached file. We should be able to come for you..." The connection closed. Renya's screen went back to the Cynet menu. Renya pounded her fist on the desk, then noticed an icon on the bottom of the screen shaped like a land formation. She clicked it. A video opened. It was Christopher, standing by an odd-shaped building.

"Welcome to Australia!" He waved, then pointed to the side of the image. A menu popped up. "This is what I've learned so far. Be sure to check out the animals. The kangaroo isn't extinct. It didn't live on Atlantis like we were taught. There's a clip of one hopping right down the road near our car."

She clicked the animal icon and then the name, kangaroo. Amazed by the size and movement of the creature, she wondered if the other animals she had been taught were extinct lived on this island as well, kept from public knowledge. She scanned their names. Another icon caught her eye. The title was, Why. She clicked it.

A document filled the screen. It started with the words, "When in the course of human events, it becomes necessary for one people to dissolve the political bands..."

A Clean Well-Lighted Cyberspace

I logged into the virtual neighborhood. Opening the Avatar window, I scrolled through the options. The defaults were like a list of Who's Who. Past the Clark Gable, Mick Jagger, Stephen Hawking (I've never seen anyone choose that option) and the like; I came to the custom option at the end of the list. If Alex hadn't talked me through it, I don't think I could have holo'ed myself into the Avatar system. The programmers sure made it was hard enough, but four holoscans and countless "Yes, I'm sure" clicks later, and I had an avatar that actually looked like myself. It's not like anyone ever bothered. With all the selections on the pull-down, making a self-image was not an option most people would choose.

I loaded my holo and made my way to Clancy's, a swanky club in the virtual center of town. The doorman was an Elvis, from the Vegas days. I guess the extra weight made him more menacing. He nodded as I floated past, into the pumping sounds and packed dance floor.

Avatars floated in, around, and through each other. I looked over the crowd. There was always the hope of seeing another real virtual, anyone who didn't look like someone from a magazine or movie. Five Tom Cruises and about ten Halle Berry's later, I adjusted my volume control.

Clancy's liked to pump out the latest commercial hits. Not commercial radio, mind you, but the latest hits from actual TV commercials. They were cranking Esoteric, from the new Target advert - the extended dance mix. Avatars swayed to the music, but all I could think of was the lady dancing with a coffee maker in the advert. I looked over to the bar, and there she was, the coffee maker lady. She had the maker sitting on the bar beside her, and a virtual smile pasted on her lips. *'Download a 10% off coupon. Ask me how'*, was glowing on the back of her shirt.

Someone floated half through me. As she passed, I looked at her back, *'Download me now'*, and her URL was emblazoned on her shirt. She was a Jessica Simpson, so I knew the site was full of dubs - famous female faces pasted onto non-famous bodies. NetBlue was all over sites like that, but you can't shut them down. All they needed were a few thousand Asian servers, and they could relay from one to the other. They were nearly impossible to trace.

I couldn't take it. I floated through and around the JoLos and George Clooneys to the door. Glancing back at Vegas Elvis, as I made my way to the street, it seemed he had a bit of a frown. You'd have to click on that, it wouldn't come natural. He could be set on auto-detect, but most people gave up on that. You spill your drink, or get an itch while VRing, and you lose that pasted-on smile. I heard some still use them for avatar 'encounters', but they usually run the script to simulate the facial expressions.

I stood on the corner. Avatars floated past, some so fast it was hard to tell if it was a Crowe or a Pitt. They flitted in and out of the shopping sites, off to the search engine stops. I used to hang out in Google's station. It was a virtual replica of Grand Central. They nearly lost the battle for rights to Yahoo!, but in the end Yahoo! went for Berlin's Lehrter Station.

I made my way down the street. The blur of passing avatars chilled me. Maybe, it was the speed at which they traveled. Maybe, it was how disconnected they were. Behind every flash of color floating past me was a human, somewhere in the world, jacked into their connection, ignoring everything in their real environment. They were sitting at a desk or café somewhere - goggles on, gloves on, alt-keying to their virtual desktop when their physical body wanted a drink of water, or clicking auto-run for a bathroom break.

I turned down an alley. Normal traffic fell away the further away from the main streets you got. Most were filled with X-rated sites, and a few hapless people who couldn't get their sites near the heavy flow streets. The further back you went, the more the irrelevancy. Now and then, someone from an alley or side street would build a site the public latched onto, then a main street would appear in front of it.

A few months ago, Catch a Mouse hit it big with the general public and got a prime location, but recently it was back to a side street. Soon, it would be an alley again - if it stayed online at all. You couldn't get a main street for the X sites. Some were suing, saying it was unfair, popular is popular regardless of content, but no one would stand up for them and say they wanted a main street, so the case was likely to founder, again.

I ducked around another corner and came to a dark side street. At the end of the block stood a small diner, large glass windows throwing their light on the empty pavement. It didn't have the stray banners and links to other places a usual back-alley joint would have. I decided it would be a good place to stop for a while, so I went in.

James Dean looked up when I came in. He was sitting with Marilyn in a booth by the door. Young Elvis was behind the counter. He looked up and smiled.

"Howdy, stranger. What can I get you?"

"Coffee." I took a seat at the counter. Young Elvis set a cup in front of me. He poured the coffee from an old-style pot. Usually, whatever you ordered would just appear, but this place was slow-mo - real time.

"Haven't seen you around," he said. "Who are you supposed to be anyway?"

"I'm me," I replied.

I took a virtual sip of my coffee and looked around. Another Marilyn was hanging all over Bogart at the corner of the counter. She had a champaign laugh, tiny bubbles of glee tumbling out of her mouth. Bogart wasn't laughing. He looked like he had clicked the *blank* option, same as me. He glanced up at me and winked. That wasn't part of the *blank*. He must have auto-detect set.

I looked around the room. There were three Elvis's, or Elvi, all from different stages. One was even in uniform. There were two Marilyns and a few Deans, but only the one Bogart. Over in a corner booth was an older man, grizzled beard, sea-captain look about him. He looked up at me, then back down to his drink. The face looked familiar, but I couldn't place it.

It used to be common to ask people who they were. Sometimes a Tom Cruise with waist-length hair was not as recognizable, but as people became used to altering the default pull-downs it went out of style, and now was almost rude to ask. Still, Young Elvis had asked me, so maybe this place was different.

I motioned to Young Elvis. He put down the glass he was cleaning and walked over. I nodded towards the sea captain.

"What's his story?"

"Custom."

"But, he looks familiar."

"I thought that too, the first time I saw him. Maybe it's a default way down the bottom of the list?" Young Elvis even had a slight drawl like the original. "I know he comes in almost every night. Always sits alone. You're a real custom, right?" I nodded. "Why?"

"I wanted to be myself."

"Be different, stand out in the crowd?"

"No. It seemed more honest."

He laughed. "No one wants to be their self for honesty's sake. You ever try a default?"

"At first. I used the Malkovich default, for about a month. I considered it a humorous play on the old movie about being him, but no one got it."

"Must have taken some work getting your holo in." He looked me over, probably trying to find an angle I'd neglected. "Is it worth it?"

"I'm more comfortable like this. What about you? Why did you pick this holo?"

"Same reason, comfort." He pulled a cup from under the counter and poured himself some coffee. "Do you get a lot of attention? People interested in the guy who isn't on the Q list?"

"Not so much. I kind of like that."

"It's easier to fade in when you go default." He looked over at a Dean.

I smiled. Customs really didn't get much attention, except from other customs. "Seems like everyone thinks if you're custom you want attention, so that's the last thing they'll give you."

He nodded in agreement. "If you want attention, go for a tattooed Mel Gibson, or a purple-eyed Clooney, and you'll get all the attention you can use." He looked up, squinting at me. "Why bother though, coming to VR, if not to meet people?"

"I guess I like to mingle. There's something very calming about walking through the throngs of clones and being almost invisible."

"You could go invisible. There's a default for that."

"It's not the same. It made me lonely - like I didn't exist at all. Did you ever try it?" He nodded, and glanced over at the old man by the window.

"What about him?" I asked. "Why do you think he comes here if he doesn't want to socialize?"

"I think he just likes to have a place to go. The faces are all familiar enough." Young Elvis smiled, looking over at the Bogart nursing his drink, with his arm around Marilyn.

"This place suits his needs. The lighting is pleasant. There isn't much of a crowd. It's peaceful and clean. As good a place as you'll find to have a quiet drink."

World, Other World

About the Author

Born in Philadelphia, Simon Just's family relocated to Virginia when Simon was nine. This meant an adjustment from exploring alleys and playing stoop-ball to exploring woods surrounding their home and digging for diamonds in the coal field under an old oak tree.

Raised by a mother who said Simon may be an alien child and should avoid any spacecrafts which beckoned, and a father who believed strongly in mechanical ingenuity, the sense of contradictions continued – city/country, imagination/science.

The dual nature of this book addresses that contrast.

World, Other World